ABANDONED

Dariah J. Rublova

Contents

3 years ago

It all started with the snick of the lighter, the bright flame popping up like magic. It used to be the lighting of a match would be enough, the smell of sulfur. But matches got wet, didn't always work. Lighters were much more portable.

He lit a crumpled rolled bit of newspaper. As the fire nibbled the edges until they turned black and curled, feeding the colorful, hot flames, he couldn't look away. Then he dropped the paper into the dumpster, breathing in those lovely gasoline fumes.

Quick quick he jumped away from the opening.

The fire caught with a breathy huff, and mushroomed up and out of the dumpster. He stayed to watch the cloud shrink back from its top height, until the fire stopped eating the gasoline and went for the real fuel, the trash bags and garbage. The gasoline can popped as the metal dented, imploding from the heat.

He had stayed to watch, but now it was time to run. Only it was too late.

A man emerged from a door, yelling for someone to call the fire department. He had an extinguisher, but he couldn't get close enough because of the heat. The man looked at him, and yelled, "Hey kid!"

But he was up and over the chain link fence and heading home. He'd gotten away with it.

He took one last look over his shoulder then ran straight into a police officer.

Chapter 1

Tyler McCracken had hoped this year would be different. First year of high school, a new school, new teachers. None of his teachers eyeing him suspiciously, wondering what he was doing in their honors class. No one looking his way when there was a fire drill.

This year was a fresh start.

His math teacher was going to be a jerk, but he was determined to ace the class despite Mr. Hill's strict homework policy and the fact that Algebra looked like another language. After receiving his first assignment in English, to read three chapters of The House of the Seven Gables by tomorrow, and a textbook in History that weighed roughly fifty pounds, it was finally time for gym class, the most important class of the day.

The gym teacher, Mr. Wheaton, wanted everyone to walk or jog laps after they filled out their information cards. Tyler stretched, then started off at a slow run. No one else was running, and he hoped that would get the coach's attention. If he could make the track team, become a varsity athlete, his father might notice him for something other than getting in trouble. Track wasn't football, the sport his dad had always talked about Tyler playing one day, but Tyler knew he could do well in track.

Running always helped him calm down. Sometimes, when he was jogging around his neighborhood with only his music for company, he'd find himself on some road he'd never been on, an hour later. His mind would go somewhere else, a calm place, a place that only fire had ever been able to take him.

If only he had his music now, he could drown out the chatter of the silly girls who were walking about as fast as his grandma. But he quickly outdistanced them. His leg muscles moved out further and further, the wind against his face. The September day was warm, and the sun felt nice on his back.

He kept sneaking peeks at Mr. Wheaton. The coach stood in the center of a throng of students who were all finishing filling out their information cards. Fine, Tyler thought. This gives me some time to warm up. By the time he finished his first lap, passing by the coach, he was ready to move up to second gear. He kicked it in right in front of the coach.

His legs felt like they were well-oiled, his feet barely touching the track. The wind ran its cold fingers through his hair. He imagined what the coach was thinking: Man, that kid's fast. I gotta get him for the track team. He could be a real asset.

Then his thoughts turned to how his dad would react. "Did you hear that, hon? We have a varsity athlete in the family. And he's taking all honors classes too. I guess Samantha's not the only good kid in the family."

Tyler couldn't help himself. He peeked back at the coach.

The guy was still talking to the other kids. A bunch of the freshman girls, the obvious cheerleader types.

Tyler tore his eyes away. Grit his teeth and really dug in. What was this guy's problem? Why couldn't he look up, just one freaking time?

"Hey. Hey, kid."

Tyler almost got whiplash from how fast he turned to see who was right behind him. Some skinny greasy kid he'd never seen before. He turned his head back forward. How did this kid catch up to him? He didn't even look winded.

"Hey, your name's Tyler, right?"

"Yeah? What of it?" Tyler puffed between breaths.

"I heard you're, like, a pyro? That you set fires and stuff?"

Tyler missed a step and stumbled. "Who told you that?" he demanded, increasing his pace. Maybe the coach will notice me now?

"Doesn't matter. So what did you burn up?"

How was this kid keeping pace with him, and still being so chatty? "I want to know who told you that."

"I heard it around. Must've been small, whatever you set on fire. Nothing too big, I don't think you've got the balls for something too big. What was it, huh? A trash can?"

Time slowed down for Tyler then. He felt his fist swinging around, weighted like a pendulum, pulling his whole body around with it. Then his fist slammed into the greasy kid's face. Something cracked under his knuckles. The kid stumbled sideways, then fell down. His hands had flown up to cover his face, and blood seeped out between his fingers. Tyler's momentum carried him back around, and he kept running. He'd barely broken stride.

He glanced over at the coach—finally he had the jerk's attention. Only now the coach was hustling across the field to help the crumpled heap of a kid back there. Tyler could practically read his thoughts.

That Tyler McCracken—he's a loose cannon. Can't have a kid like that on the team.

***

Tyler stood at the kitchen counter, tapping his fingers against the pink slip of paper proclaiming his suspension.

His mother bustled around, preparing dinner. His father sat at the table, reading the paper. Both of them must have seen the pink slip he'd left on the counter when he got home from school, but neither had come up to his room, where he had been studiously doing his homework, since they had come home from work.

So, he had gone downstairs to face the music.

His mom was pissed. The way she was matter-of-factly chopping up onions and peppers, her movements brisk and vigorous. His dad was more difficult to read – he sat at the table, his face buried in the newspaper. Now his mom was pulling out pans and banging them around. The thing about his mom, she wasn't going to say anything if she could help it.

"Aren't you even going to yell at me?" he asked finally.

"What's the point of that? You don't listen to us."

Part of him wanted to yell, That's not true! But he couldn't think of one time since the fire thing three years ago that he'd listened to them. His sister Sam, he listened to her. But she actually treated him like a human being and not some big disappointment.

Instead he said, "You're supposed to yell at me."

His father turned a page in the paper. "I'm sure you had a good reason to hit that other kid."

Tyler whirled around. "No, I didn't have a good reason! There's never a good reason to hit someone!"

"Then why did you hit him, if that's how you feel?"

Same even-tempered tone, like he was talking about the weather.

"He was pissing me off! I didn't even think about it before I did it. But it was wrong, and you're my parents, and you're supposed to teach me right from wrong!"

"Oh, so now it's our fault?" his mother said.

"No!" How did this always get turned around? "I just mean, you're supposed to ground me or something."

His dad turned another page in the paper. "Fine. You're grounded."

"Fine!"

On his way out of the kitchen, he slammed his fist into the wall.

He sat in his room for only a minute before his father creaked up the stairs. From the defeated tone in his voice, it was clear his mother had pushed his father to come up and talk to him.

"Tyler, come on, let's talk about this."

His dad's footsteps stopped outside his door. Through the wood his father said, "Tyler, your mother and I love you no matter what you do. It hurts us to see you sabotage yourself."

Tyler thought about opening the door and talking to his dad, then put on his sneakers and grabbed his phone and earbuds.

"You need to talk about what's making you so angry—"

His father looked surprised when Tyler yanked open the door. The surprise helped Tyler to slip past him and down the stairs. "Where are you going?"

Tyler ignored him and headed down the stairs. He had opened the front door when his father caught up to him and slammed the door closed. "Tyler, you're not leaving."

"I'm going for a run, that's all. Don't worry, I'm not going to set anything on fire."

His father caught his arm and said, "Tyler, wait a minute—"

Tyler jerked his arm away. "Leave me alone!" He ran through the house to the back door, where he let himself out and took off running into the woods.

Chapter 2

Tyler stopped thinking, let his muscles work, stretch, and fly. He loved this feeling, like he could run away from everything. Nothing could stop him. He was the fastest person in the world. All he needed was to be alone.

There was still enough light at this hour, but the clouds were moving in, and before he knew it, fat drops of rain started to fall. He kept running, enjoying how the water made him feel like he was moving even faster, but eventually thunder rolled and the downpour started.

He'd been running full out for over half an hour, and his anger was spent now anyway, so he slowed down and started looking for a tree or a rock or something, anything, that might give him some shelter from the rain. Nothing but pine trees as far as he could see. He ran faster, his sneakers slipping a bit on the wet pine needles, and stumbled onto a dirt road.

It was barely a road. Weeds up to his knees, growing in a twin set of ruts that looked like tires had last come up this way a hundred years ago. It was pretty unmistakable as a road, though. Straight, and cleared of the dense trees. And up ahead, something gray and white that contrasted with the greens and browns of the forest.

A house.

Tyler headed for it, wondering what he might say to the people who lived there. "Hey, would you mind letting a random, possibly delinquent, kid like myself in to wait out this rainstorm in your house?" Yeah, right. But his clothes were drenched and he could feel rivulets running from his hair all the way down his back.

As Tyler got closer he could see that the house was dark, and shrouded by trees and scrub brush. The road was so bumpy he kept stumbling and slipping as loose dirt turned to mud. Where the driveway should have been were overgrown bushes. Tyler picked his way through the sapling trees and weeds and finally got to the front door.

The house had once been white, but most of the paint had chipped off, leaving the house a weathered brown, with spots of white. A little addition on the side, some kind of a three-season porch, clung to the side of the building with pieces of the roof. The door to the porch was missing and a variety of trash bags were piled up inside, covered by a layer of pine needles and leaves that had probably been there since last fall, or the fall before that.

Tyler stared up at the black windows, squinting through the rain. The windows were the old kind his mom liked, with sixteen little panes of glass, the kind his father had removed from their house over the summer. "They're not very economical," he told her when she had complained.

"They had character," his mother had replied, but there wasn't anything she could do about it then, because his father had already bought new windows and they were supposed to save them a bundle on heating.

Most of the panes were intact, but a few had cracked, and some had disappeared altogether. The windowless frames stared back at him like empty eyes.

No one could possibly live here, Tyler told himself. Still, he hesitated at the threshold, even though the door was actually stuck open.

"Hello?" he called into the house. He knocked on the door, as loud as a wet fist on damp wood could. "Anybody home?"

He listened for an answer, but the rain was deafening, drumming on the roof. He hoped there wasn't some homeless guy holed up in here, some old pervert just waiting for a nice young kid like Tyler to walk into his lair...

Ridiculous, Tyler thought, and pushed at the door.

Green paint flaked off on his hand, but pushing hadn't moved the swollen door one inch. He pushed harder, then pushed with both hands. Finally a budge. Another push, and the door opening was enough for him to squeeze through.

He stood in a kitchen. As he wrung the excess water from his clothes onto the curling linoleum, he took in the ancient appliances with their big rounded handles and knobs, the trash and leaves on the floor. Curtains laced with holes attempted to conceal the window over the sink, which had rust stains running down from the faucet.

Tyler walked through the kitchen, marveling at all the things left behind. On the counter, underneath layers of dust, sat an ancient toaster and a moldy carton of milk. The carton looked soft, in a gross way. Like it would dissolve into a gelatinous mass if Tyler was to touch it. In his sixth grade history class he had learned how the people in Pompeii hadn't had time to escape the volcano, how they'd run out of their houses in the middle of dinner to try to get away. They'd found houses perfectly preserved under the lava—people too, only at first they thought there were just big air bubbles, but when they filled the bubble with plaster, the shape they came out with was the shape of a person, curled up, who'd been instantly turned to ash by the molten lava.

Tyler shuddered.

The place might be abandoned now, but people had been here since that original family had moved on. Beer cans, bottles, and the charred remains of leaves and trash littered the scorched linoleum. Tyler kicked a rusting can with an old fashioned logo - Rondo Premium Citrus Soda - he'd never even heard of that kind.

In the living room, the wallpaper had begun to peel off, some god awful olive print. Some of the exposed plaster had cracked off of the walls, leaving bare slats. On one side of the room was a crumbling fireplace, filled with leaves and branches and burned up trash. He wandered close, observing those ashy, charcoaled bits of debris. The last fire hadn't been very recent. The chimney was probably clogged with either dead leaves or bats or bird nests, and if he started a fire now, the smoke would only cycle back into the house. The whole place would burn down, all this dead and rotting wood would go up in flames so fast...

Tyler swallowed thickly. He turned away, put his back to the fireplace, and assessed the rest of the room.

As for furniture, there was a sofa Tyler would never be able to bring himself to sit on, unless he had one of those plastic covers his great-grandparents used to cover their furniture. The scratchy brown fabric had been stained repeatedly and had the same gross softness as the milk carton in the kitchen.

He looked up at the ceiling, suddenly realizing that the house was probably structurally unsound. There were leaks, none dripping at the moment, but once the water trickled down, they'd probably correspond to the giant discolored stains in the ceiling where paint had peeled away and crackled down to the floor like snow, and the water leaking from them would most likely hit more than one of the random tin cans and cracked plastic buckets scattered around on the floor. Unfortunately, most of the buckets were already full, and had overflowed and caused moldy splotches to grow around them on the hardwood floor. Maybe once it had been hardwood. Now it was soft, rotten wood.

Tyler stepped carefully.

The Oriental carpet in the center of the room was caked in mud, paint, and plaster bits. The rug might have originally been red. Or brown.

There were stairs, but Tyler wasn't sure about heading up there. They looked all right, though. Sturdy. Sturdier than the living room floor, but it was dark, and he didn't want to chance it.

He didn't see the crates set up in the corner until he turned around. Two plastic milk crates, with a makeshift table made from a scrap of plywood between them. A couple of playing cards lingered on the table top.

Tyler stepped closer and picked up one of the cards. Dust covered it, and it was floppy, not like the plastic coated cards his family had that were so slippery and hard to shuffle. He felt like he could rip this card in half by looking at it. There were more beer cans here, crushed, and empty glass bottles of Jack Daniels.

Maybe some homeless guy had been waiting here. Him and his friend, playing cards. Good thing for Tyler they left about ten years ago.

Tyler took a seat on one of the milk crates and tried to believe his good luck. This was exactly what he needed. A place to go where he could be alone and at peace, where he didn't have to think about the way his parents had given up on him.

Of course, he'd had a place like this once. Four years ago, when the McCrackens lived in Lowell, Tyler had found an abandoned warehouse while riding his bike around the city. On those days when he didn't feel like hanging around with his friends spraying graffiti on the sides of buildings but didn't want to go home where his perfect sister would be done her homework and his mom would be complaining about his dad working late yet again, Tyler went to the warehouse. He did his own graffiti there, more abstract and artistic than the initials and slurs he'd paint with his friends. These were murals, big beautiful murals.

At first the fires kept him warm as the season changed from fall to winter. He used a lighter he'd found in a gutter and burned the trash and leaves and old newspapers that filled every corner of the warehouse. The warehouse was made of brick and cinderblock; he'd been sure it was safe. Fireplaces made out of the same stuff.

That day he had arrived at the warehouse, his stomach churning and his teeth grinding. Now he couldn't remember why he was so angry, but the fire seemed to help. He fed it fuel until it was as big as a bonfire. The flames were near to licking the support beams over Tyler's head before he heard that ominous creak in the floor. Wind blowing in through the broken windows whipped the fire into a frenzy and Tyler got scared and ran. He tore off on his bike, thankful that no one was around, and watched from a nearby hill as the fire destroyed half the building. The fire trucks arrived a short time later. The whole time his heart was racing, but in a good way. His anger was gone, replaced by this thrill.

That was his first big fire. Only much later, the next time school made him mad, did he regret the fire. He'd lost his hiding place. Which led to things like the dumpster, and getting arrested.

He'd never told anyone about the warehouse fire, not even his therapist.

Tyler felt more than heard the rain let up outside. It was a feeling of things coming back to life again, instead of hiding from the storm.

He could hear things now, something dripping upstairs, the house creaking and settling around him. One day, maybe a hundred or three hundred years from now, maybe the house would settle right down into the ground, and disappear. Weeds would grow right over it and no one would ever know it had been there.

Or that Tyler had been here.

By the time Tyler returned home, his anger was spent. It was a good long hike home from the abandoned house, and he was wet and uncomfortable and tired. He kicked his shoes off at the door and went up to take a long hot shower.

"You need to fix the holes in the wall," his mother said as he walked through the living room to the stairs.

"I know," he replied, but all he was thinking about was the abandoned house.

Chapter 3

In-house suspension meant sitting in the same room all day with the same kids, while the teachers traded out places behind the desk at the front of the room. Tyler looked at the three other kids in the room, relieved he wasn't the only one who got in trouble on the first day of school.

Mike Beaumont, the son of his mother's coworker and the only person Tyler knew before school started, had told him all about the kid sitting near the window. According to Mike, Ben Simms had once brought a homemade machete to school, and another time, a fresh animal pelt, and spent most of his days in the suspension room.

The other two kids must have gotten into a fight with each other. One of them slumped in his seat, casting occasional glares at the other kid, who had on a black hooded sweatshirt. He had the hood pulled down to hide his split lip and the bruise on his jaw.

Tyler sat near Ben and pulled out his math textbook. The morning bell had rung but no one else was doing any work. They were all just sitting there, even the teacher. He was the only one with a textbook out.

Ben was chewing on a toothpick. He nodded at Tyler.

"Hey, what's up," Tyler said, trying to look cool. There was no way to look cool while doing homework. It was impossible.

"You're not allowed to do homework in here," Ben said.

Tyler stared at him.

"He's right," said the teacher, who finally stood up. He smoothed his tie over his dress shirt, making sure it lined up with the buttons. "You are not allowed to do homework during in-house suspension, because you're earning a zero for the day. That's what suspension means."

What a jerk, Tyler thought, as the teacher walked over to the cabinet and pulled out a stack of booklets.

"In lieu of doing homework, you can all read over the school rules." He started passing out the booklets, letting the full weight of each slap onto the desk tops. When he got to the desk of the kid in the hooded sweatshirt, he stopped. "And for those of you already familiar with the school rules, you can start on copying them down, word for word."

The kid in the black sweatshirt didn't even look up.

Tyler put away his homework and opened the booklet.

"I expect complete silence. Anyone who talks without raising his hand can expect a half-hour detention at the end of the day—"

"Hey, sorry I'm late!"

Tyler didn't have to look to know that voice. He gritted his teeth and glared at the rule book.

"And you are?"

"Danny Krull. What's your name?"

Tyler had to quirk a smile at that. Then Danny – the kid he had punched yesterday, the kid responsible for Tyler getting suspended – plopped himself into the seat right next to Tyler and grinned at him.

Tyler quickly looked down, glaring at his desktop.

"I am Mr. Edward. May I ask why you are tardy?"

Danny laughed like he just couldn't hold it in. "Tardy? Are you for real?" Danny wheezed between guffaws. It almost made Tyler want to laugh with him.

"What is so funny, Mr. Krull?"

Danny cleared his throat. "Um, nothing. I got lost on the way here."

Mr. Edward sighed, then got another rule book and put it on Danny's desk. "I will let it slide this time, Mr. Krull. In the future, however, I will not be so kind. To reiterate the rules of in-house suspension, which you missed: You are not allowed to do homework. You are not allowed to talk. You are to read the rule book, and when you are finished reading, you may copy the rule book, or write an essay reflecting on why you were suspended."

"That's bullshit!" Danny said.

Why can't he keep his mouth shut? Tyler thought.

"Mr. Krull, you have just earned yourself a detention for profanity."

"No, man, for real. This is stupid. We're at school, but we can't do homework? I knew I shoulda skipped." Danny flopped back in his seat, crossing his arms.

"This is what is called punishment, Mr. Krull," droned Mr. Edward. "Now, if you wish to avoid any more detentions, you will remain silent."

Surprisingly, no one said a word for about fifteen solid minutes. Tyler tried to concentrate on the rule book, but couldn't get past the school's mission statement: "We strive to provide our students with the fullest education in accordance with MCAS standards blah blah blah."

His mind kept wandering to the abandoned house. After school, he was going to go there. He still remembered how the house had made him feel: calm, welcome. Like it wanted him there, somehow. It had felt more like home than his actual home.

Looking down, he realized he had been staring at the first page of the rule book for a while now. He turned the page, then immediately thought about how he could fix the house up a little. Really make it his home. And he wanted to explore the upstairs...

"God, this is so boring."

Danny said it in one quiet breath, but Mr. Edward's head snapped up like a snake fixing on its prey.

"Mr. Krull! Another detention!"

Danny flew forward in his chair, slamming his head against the desk, and clenched his fists up next to his face. "...aarrggh..."

"I realize that you are a freshman, Mr. Krull, and that you are a transfer student. This is because I, unlike other teachers, read the files of the students in my suspension hall."

Tyler's stomach sank. Here he was, thinking high school teachers were too busy to read their students' files. All along they knew. He bet Mr. Edward had told the other teachers already: Watch out for this one! A real pyromaniac here!

"Apparently the discipline at your school in Lowell was a bit lax. Here, we take threats of violence against teachers very seriously. And although you were on the receiving end of the attack by Mr. McCracken here—" there were sounds of approval from the other kids, and Mr. Edward raised his voice to compensate, "—it takes two to tango. Therefore, you are here for more than one reason, as are most of your colleagues. However, you do not hear them chattering away."

Danny lifted his head and gave Mr. Edward a look that said, What part of my primal scream of rage sounds like chattering to you?

Tyler had to stifle a giggle.

The bell rang for the end of first period, and Tyler moved to get up automatically.

"Not quite yet, Mr. McCracken. You've got another seven periods before you'll get to leave."

Tyler sank back down into his uncomfortable plastic chair.

It was a long nine minutes before the next teacher came to relieve the impenetrable Mr. Edward. "Hey, guys," said the short, brown-haired woman who hurried in, burdened with a stack of papers and a crammed tote bag.

"Miss Donoghue. Punctual as ever," said Mr. Edward dryly as he left the room.

Miss Donoghue didn't even acknowledge him. She threw her stuff on the desk. "Okay, let's have names." She pointed to the kid in the creaking chair.

"Jay," he said.

"Oh, wait. Hold on, hold on." Miss Donoghue rifled through the papers and pulled one out. "Jay, Jay, Jay... Oh! Jason Hodgkins. Next?"

"Adam Fritz," muttered hooded sweatshirt kid.

"Adam. Okay. You?"

"Ben."

"Okay. And you?" She pointed at Tyler.

"Tyler McCracken."

"And that means you are Daniel. Great! Everyone's here! Who wants to do some icebreakers?"

Everyone else must have been looking at Miss Donoghue the same way Tyler was, because she immediately followed her suggestion with, "Okay, well, feel free to do homework or whatever," and went behind the desk and pulled out her lesson book.

Tyler dragged out his history book to read the chapters. Finally he could get something accomplished.

"Hey. Tyler."

Tyler clenched his jaw and did not look up.

Danny started in with an exaggerated, "Psssst."

Miss Donoghue didn't seem to care that Danny was talking. Tyler turned his head levelly to look at Danny Krull.

"What."

"Remember what I was asking you yesterday?" Danny's eyes flicked toward Miss Donoghue.

Tyler tried to put as much of an edge to his voice as he could. "Yes?" Maybe Danny would get the hint that Tyler didn't want to discuss his past.

"So I was thinking, maybe you want to hang out after school."

He had punched this kid in the face yesterday, hadn't he? Yes, Danny's nose was swollen. He hadn't imagined the blood.

"Don't you, like, have detention for the next three months after school?" Tyler asked, going back to his homework.

"Maybe this weekend?" Danny asked after a few moments.

"Yeah, right." Tyler meant it to sound sarcastic, but it didn't quite come out that way.

"Cool! So, like, you wanna give me your phone number?"

Not really, he thought, but something wouldn't let him say it. The kid sounded so... so... desperate. Tyler scribbled his number on a scrap of paper and handed it to him.

Moments later he realized that he could have given Danny a wrong number. But he didn't want to think about Danny calling that number, and the way Danny would feel listening to a recorded voice saying the number had been disconnected, or a stranger answering and saying they'd never heard of anyone named Tyler and never to call back again. And then the way Danny would look the next time they passed in the hall.

"Cool, man, cool," Danny was saying.

Suddenly Tyler remembered what Mr. Edward had said, that Danny was from Lowell. Tyler looked at Danny out of the corner of his eye. No way could he have forgotten someone like Danny.

"This is so great!"

Tyler and Danny both turned to look at Miss Donoghue, who had her hands clasped in front of her. Her eyes were shining.

"You two are friends now! The jock and the delinquent! This is just like The Breakfast Club!"

Tyler didn't know what The Breakfast Club was, but he was pretty sure he didn't want to be a part of it. Especially if he didn't know whether he was the jock or the delinquent.

Chapter 4

After school, Tyler dropped off his backpack, popped in his earbuds, and as a second thought, tucked the book for English class into the front pocket of his hoodie. He scrawled a note to his parents before heading into the woods at an easy jog.

The sunlight filtered through the trees and his sneakers pounded the damp earth, hurrying toward his destination. All day long the house had squirreled its way into his thoughts. The memory of how he'd gotten there was muddled in anger, and he hoped he remembered the way. But soon running overtook him, bringing in calm the way he loved.

He nearly ran right past the dirt road - his mind had wandered away with everything that had happened with Danny during in-house suspension. He checked the time. He'd only been running for 22 minutes. It had seemed like much longer yesterday.

Tyler jogged up the hill toward the house. The door to the kitchen was still wedged open. He shoved the door closed behind him, then surveyed the kitchen, the leaves and trash all over the floor. This place could use a good sweeping, he thought, then decided to check the closets and cabinets for a broom. He pulled at the little handle on the closet beside the front door a few times before it swung open suddenly and something scurried out.

He heard himself shrieking like a little girl as he danced around trying to see what it was. He glimpsed the bushy tail end of a squirrel as it scurried out of a window.

"I'm an idiot," he said, trying to laugh it off, but the house only answered with silence. He cleared his throat, looked at the ceiling. "Sorry."

No one answered.

Feeling stupid, he returned to the closet. Some kind of nest in there, with a little chewed-out hole in back leading outside. There was a broom in here, but it was useless—the squirrels must have chewed off the straw part to make their nest, leaving just the wooden pole. There was a dustpan and brush hanging from nails on the side, and an ancient bottle of furniture polish covered in oily dust. Again Tyler wondered why someone would leave this stuff behind. Although the more he thought about it, if he had to leave in a rush, he wouldn't think twice about leaving behind some old cleaning junk.

He reached for the dustpan before realizing that he didn't have a trash bag, which would make cleaning up pointless. He closed the door and opted instead to explore the rest of the house.

The bathroom was pretty clean, considering. He'd expected it to smell, but there wasn't any water in the toilet. The tub had some rust stains, and a little dirty pool of water with leaves and plaster floating in it. When he looked up at the ceiling, there was a large, dark brown stain spreading out from a corner of the ceiling. The plaster looked so rotted he took a step back, as though it might crumble down on him at any second.

When he moved, something out of the corner of his eye moved with him.

Fear froze him in place for a moment. Forcing himself to breathe, he took a tentative step forward and jumped at what he saw.

His own face looked back at him from a metal medicine cabinet hanging over the sink. He allowed himself a nervous laugh, then grasped the edge of the mirror and eased it open.

With a long rusty creak, the cabinet revealed a variety of old-timey personal care products. A hard-as-rock tube of toothpaste with a metal tab at the bottom to roll it up, accompanied by a can of shaving cream and a rusty razor. An brown prescription bottle—Tyler shook it only to find it empty. Whoever had used the house to drink and play cards had probably taken the remaining pills. The label was worn, but a few of the typewritten letters were still legible: b, r, double ll's.

There was a hairbrush, too, with hairs still in it. Long blonde hairs.

Tyler closed the cabinet and headed to the next room.

At one point, this room must have been some kind of office, way before computers. The papers scattered all over the floor surrounded a wooden desk. Most of the books still sat in order on the bookshelves that lined the back wall. He stepped over the papers to see the titles. Moldy romance novels from the fifties, a few books about real estate law, architecture, boring junk. More books lay on the floor, with pages torn out.

Tyler opened a few desk drawers. Nothing. He moved upstairs.

The stairs looked sketchy, but all of them held. The second floor was much smaller than he'd imagined. There were two doors on his right and one on his left.

All of the doors were closed.

He opened the first one on his right. This one appeared to be the master bedroom. A big bed with sloping head and footboards dominated the middle of the room. A wardrobe stood off to the side, and a little table sat under a window. Unlike the rooms downstairs, this one was nearly intact. There were still sheets and a comforter on the bed, pillows with neatly arranged shams underneath a layer of dust. The rugs looked bleached by the sunlight but otherwise almost clean.

Tyler moved to step over the threshold to the room, but something stopped him. It took him a minute to understand why he was reluctant to enter. This room was like a tomb. How had those archeologists entered King Tut's tomb? How they could have felt so entitled to disturb what had been at rest for so many years? This room had only been abandoned for maybe one hundred years, and he couldn't bring himself to do it.

He stepped back, shut the door.

When he opened the second door on the right, he couldn't see anything. Slowly the windowless interior came into view from the dim light in the hallway, which came from a hole in the roof. A twin-size bed, with a bare mattress. Next to the bed there was a table, with a kerosene lamp and a book on top. Tyler leaned in to see the book. The light glinted weakly off of a golden cross on the cover. A Bible.

The bed and the table, that was it. It was the size of a large closet. With no windows. Tyler looked back at the bed, and saw a large, dark stain marring the striped ticking on the mattress.

Suddenly he felt sick. He wanted to shut the door and never go back there again. Both of his hands were digging into the door frame. He tried to pull back out of the room and felt himself

stick

then he pushed with all his strength and pulled himself the hell out of there.

He stood staring at the black hole of the room. He needed to shut the door. He couldn't leave it open. The lurching in his stomach told him he really was going to be sick. But he had to shut that door first.

The darkness in the corners weren't made of shadows. The darkness was alive, overpowering the light and crawling toward him. It crept across the rotting floorboards, enveloped that stained mattress, steadily making its way to his feet.

He watched it, his mind a blank slate of horror.

How long had he been standing here staring at that empty, dark doorway, feeling the bile rising in the back of his throat? He reached forward cat-quick and grabbed the knob and pulled. For a second he felt something—someone?—pulling back, and he almost let go in surprise. But then the door slammed shut.

Tyler blinked. The sunlight streaming in through the room took away the terror he had just felt. He was jumping at shadows. The door was just sticky, like all the other doors were stuck. As he turned away, he kept that closed door in his peripheral vision. The dark slit between the door and the floor especially.

The door to the third bedroom, the one room on the left, was open.

This was it, this was the pull he'd felt all day. The sun was streaming in through the remains of the lace curtains in the windows, and the room was warmer than any of the other rooms in the house.

There was a brass bed, a little white bureau with a vanity mirror. Tyler stepped inside. Those guys, those poker-players and drunks, had been here. They had dragged mattress to the floor where it now bled stuffing and coils from several deep gashes. A beer bottle lay shattered in the corner. There were stains on the pink and white braided rug—not ominous stains like the one on that bed in that room Tyler didn't want to think about—lighter stains, water or maybe spilled beer. He hoped it wasn't urine.

A plastic horse lay on the floor by the window. Tyler picked it up. It was a pinto, white with faded brown spots, a Breyer. One of the front legs had broken off.

Still carrying the horse, Tyler wandered over to the bureau and touched the pink flowers painted on the white-painted wood. The mirror was cracked.

This had been some little girl's room. Tyler's fists balled up at those degenerates who had broken in here and destroyed everything they could. There was no need for this kind of destruction.

He set the horse carefully down on the bureau top, balancing it so it managed to stand without the leg, and moved to the mattress. He lifted one side, and flipped it back onto the bed frame so that the damaged parts were on the bottom. The new top side of the mattress still looked a bit lumpy, but it was clean. He sat down and bounced up and down. Not too bad. He pulled his copy of The House of Seven Gables out from where it was digging into his ribs and rolled onto his side.

Hours later, judging from the way the sun had slid across the room, Tyler closed the book and stretched. Normally reading was such a chore, especially books by dead white guys like Nathaniel Hawthorne. In this old, dead place, though, the writing fit.

He tucked his book away and headed out. Only when he had crossed the road and was jogging home did he start to worry about what he would tell his parents about where he'd been.

Chapter 5

Despite winning eight out of ten sprint matches during tryouts and coming in third in the mile, Tyler hadn't made the track team, which soured Tyler's day in suspension. Everything Danny did annoyed him. It was all Danny's fault. If Danny hadn't brought up Tyler's past that first day of school, Tyler would have made the team. And he wouldn't have been suspended.

Tyler hadn't told his parents he was trying out for track, and he didn't have much to say about school, which made family dinner on Friday evening a quiet and awkward affair. Tyler chewed his food and listened to his parents chew theirs.

Then the phone rang. His mom jumped up to answer it—she'd been waiting for Sam to call since she left for college two weeks ago. By the way her face fell immediately after answering, Tyler knew it wasn't Sam.

She held the phone out to Tyler. "It's for you."

Mike Beaumont was the only one who had his number. Probably Mike was calling to tell Tyler the homework. Still, talking to Mike was better than the silence.

He accepted the phone. "Hello?"

"Hey, Ty! What's up?"

He struggled to place that voice. Who had ever called him "Ty"?

"Who is this?" he asked.

"Duh, it's Danny. You gave me your phone number the other day?"

"Oh. Yeah." Tyler wondered if his face had the same disappointed cast his mother's now wore.

"Wanna come over to my house tomorrow? I live on Sorrel Hill Road, do you know where that is?"

Tyler did know where that was. Apparently, Danny lived only a few streets over from Tyler. "Yeah, I know where that is."

"Cool. Maybe we could meet at Dunkin Donuts and get some coffee, then head up to my place. You got a bike?"

Dunkin Donuts was across from the high school, which was only about a ten-minute walk from Tyler's house. The gears in Tyler's head started clicking. "Sure. What time do you want to meet?"

"Eleven? I get up real early but most people like to sleep in, I guess."

For a moment before he said, "Okay," Tyler realized he could have said he was busy. He could have given a thousand different excuses. But he also wanted to know how Danny knew about his past.

"Great, see you tomorrow!'

Tyler exhaled in relief when he hung up the phone. If he got there way early, he could even pretend he lived down by where Mike lived, and Danny would never know he lived so close.

Tyler was so relieved that he didn't notice the way his parents were staring at him curiously until after he had shoveled some more of his dinner into his mouth. "What?" he asked through a mouthful.

"Who was that on the phone?" his mother asked.

Her tone made Tyler wonder if this was a trick question. "A kid from school."

"What kid? Have we met him before?"

"No, he's just this kid..." Tyler couldn't exactly tell her how he had met Danny. "I think he moved here over the summer."

"What's his name?"

Tyler paused at his mother's questioning. She was pissed about something, and if he accused her of interrogating him, she'd only get more angry. Best to just answer the questions. "Danny Krull."

"I don't recall anyone by that name buying a house this summer." Tyler's mother worked at the real estate agency in the center of town.

Tyler shrugged.

"And where did you meet this boy? In-house suspension?"

"Why would you think that?" Tyler asked.

"Because you've been suspended for the majority of your freshman year thus far," his father remarked dryly.

Tyler resisted the urge to growl, and instead put more food in his mouth. He hoped his inability to answer would stop his mother from asking more questions.

"And you're planning on hanging out with this boy?"

Tyler nodded.

"Well." She looked at his father, who looked up from his meal like a dumb cow. "You should think twice about befriending some boy you met in suspension hall. I don't want you slipping back into your old behavior patterns."

Terminology like what his therapist used to say all the time, like he had any clue what "behavior patterns" she meant. Setting fires? Skipping school? Punching kids?

He swallowed the lump of tasteless food in his mouth and said, "I don't see what's wrong with making a new friend." It was painful to have to resort to that argument, when he didn't even want Danny to know where he lived.

"All I'm saying, Tyler, is that keeping company with some delinquent—"

" 'Some delinquent'? Who are you talking about? Me or him?"

The words erupted out of him, and it felt good. He'd felt like a volcano ready to blow for the past 5,000 years.

His mother's face shut down. Collapsed.

"I should've known that's what you still think of me," Tyler said, the growl now entering his voice. He stood up. "I'm going for a run."

Of course he went to the abandoned house.

***

After spending a few hours at the house last night, he returned knowing he needed to make amends with his parents, even if he still didn't want to talk to them, so he got up early on Saturday to patch the hole he'd punched in the wall the other day.

He scraped some plaster over the screening and, knowing it would take a while for it to set before he could sand it down, took off on his bike without telling his parents where he was going. He wasn't ready to talk to them yet. And he still had to beat Danny to Dunkin Donuts.

Checking to make sure he had enough time, he headed down Proctor Road, then circled back to Main Street, so it would look like he was coming from the opposite direction. This way, if Danny happened to be early as well, he would have no idea where Tyler really lived.

His bike had rusted a bit from being in the garage for the past three years, and even though he was in good shape from running, he was sweaty and his face red when he pulled up at quarter to eleven. He had plenty of time to catch his breath. He parked his bike in front and pulled some crumpled dollar bills out of his pocket. A Coolatta would hit the spot right now.

"I thought you'd never get here." Tyler almost jumped out of his skin as Danny emerged from Dunkin Donuts sucking on a huge iced coffee. The top of the cup was about as big as Danny's face.

"Geez, what size did you get?"

"The biggest size they had. I can drink a 64 oz. Big Gulp in like two seconds."

No wonder Danny was always twitching around. "Where's your bike?"

"Oh, it's in the back. I asked them if I could keep my bike in their kitchen so no one would steal it. Since there's no bike rack here."

Tyler could only imagine the looks on the staff's faces when Danny asked them to keep his bike in their kitchen. He supposed in Lowell that might have been a necessary precaution, but this place wasn't exactly crawling with bike thieves.

"Anyway, we can hang here for a bit. I don't think I can drink this while I ride my bike."

"Cool," Tyler said, again remembering how hot he was. As soon as he started walking, his leg muscles burned. He hoped he'd be able to get to Danny's house. It was mostly uphill from here.

Tyler ordered his drink, a fruity mango-strawberry mix. He had to wait behind a family of six ordering all sorts of donuts and sweetened drinks. By the time he got back to where Danny was sitting, Danny had downed three-quarters of his coffee and was pinching the bridge of his nose with his eyes shut.

"Brain freeze brain freeze brainfreeze," Danny hissed. Then he screwed up his face and shook his head and opened his eyes. "All better," he said to Tyler.

Tyler sipped at his drink.

"When I was riding my bike around earlier, you know, cuz I just like to ride around and explore, you know? And you know what I found?"

For a moment Tyler worried that Danny found the house.

"I found this cool cemetery. It's, like, really old. There was a funeral or something going on, all these people in black crying and stuff, and a hearse. They've probably cleared out by now. Wanna go?"

Like Tyler had never been to a cemetery before. However, anything would be better than sitting here wondering what to say to the kid who he'd sat next to for the past three days, doing nothing. "Sure, why not."

Danny couldn't wait for Tyler to finish his Coolatta, so Tyler tried to hold it and steer his rusty bike one-handed. He wobbled a bit, trying to get the hang of it, then Danny came whipping out from the back of the Dunkin Donuts. He skidded to a stop in front of Tyler, and looked at Tyler and his bike and his Coolatta skeptically.

"That's not gonna work, dude."

"I just have to—"

"Naw, dude, suck it down and let's go."

"What?"

"Drink it. Man up. We don't have all day."

He didn't like Danny bossing him around, yet Tyler knew it wasn't going to work, especially not with the way his gears were all rusted. He put the straw in his mouth and started drinking.

"Drink, drink, drink," Danny chanted.

About five sips in, Tyler got a headache.

"Wuss! Keep going!"

Tyler grit his teeth. A runt like Danny calling him a wuss? He sucked down the rest of the drink, ignoring the headache, and the brain freeze, and the way his throat felt ice cold. He kept slurping until all he could hear was the slurping noises from the straw hitting the bottom of the plastic cup.

"Yeah! Now let's go!"

Tyler walked over to throw the cup away, feeling sick. When he turned back around, he saw Danny already out of the parking lot.

He clambered onto his bike and followed. Already he knew this was a badidea.

Chapter 6

About a million hills later, the black wrought iron fence of the cemetery came into view. Danny leaned his bike carefully against the fence and wrapped a chain around it. Tyler dropped his on the ground and leaned himself against the fence to catch his breath.

"Boy, you're out of shape," Danny remarked.

Tyler glared at him.

"Come on, let's go." Instead of walking to the entrance, Danny hopped over the fence. Tyler dragged himself over and staggered after him.

"Look at all these old tombstones."

They were in the old section of the cemetery, where the town's ancestors were buried. Tyler peered at the crumbling tombstones. The dates went back to the 1700s. Instead of angels, little skulls with wings were etched above the names.

As he followed Danny up another hill, Danny gave him a tour. "See that huge pile of flowers over there? That's where the funeral was this morning. Probably some old person. There were a lot of old people at the funeral."

Tyler paused to brace his hands on his knees and catch his breath. Some of the tombstones stood half-buried, like the ground was slowly devouring them. Just like the abandoned house collapsing in toward the ground.

"Hey Tyler, watch this."

Tyler looked up in time to see Danny do a karate kick at a tombstone. The shale-soft stone snapped off and toppled to the ground.

"What are you doing?" Tyler yelled.

A blackbird in the tree above flew away with a loud ca-caw!

Danny shrugged. "What?"

"You can't go around kicking over tombstones. You'll get arrested."

Danny slung his arm around Tyler's shoulders. "That's the beauty of doing things in the daytime. No one suspects anything can go wrong with the sun shining."

Tyler shrugged off Danny's arm. "No, really. You shouldn't do that."

Even as the words came out of his mouth, Tyler couldn't think of any reasons to object to what Danny had done.

"These people have been dead for centuries. Nobody's gonna care."

"But... they're historical markers, or whatever." Then again, there was little difference between his fires and this. No, he was right to be angry. He'd only been burning trash. People burned trash all the time. Breaking someone's tombstone was disrespectful.

"Yeah, whatever." Danny took a flying leap and kicked over another one.

Tyler jammed his fists into his pockets and headed toward the newer section of the cemetery, the sound of more breaking stone behind him.

These markers were sturdier. He started to slow down and read the dates, running the numbers through his head.

1880-1965, that guy had lived a good long time.

1895-1919, he'd probably died during World War I. He had a flag in front of his grave, definitely a veteran.

1922-1936.

Someone who had died when they were fourteen, his age. He glanced at the name. A girl. Right in the middle of the Great Depression. That sucked, she didn't even know that the economy got better. Maybe she had even starved to death because there wasn't enough food. No, that didn't really happen, did it? There were a lot of orphans then, though.

Her parents were buried on either side of her, but they had died decades later.

"Hey, wait up!"

Danny galloped over, splashing through puddles. "There's a freaking mausoleum over there! It's locked, but maybe I can pick it."

"She was our age when she died," Tyler said, pointing.

The tombstone was unadorned, only simple flowery scrollwork around the letters that spelled her name: Ellen Miriam Birdsall.

"Miriam. That's, like, a grandmother's name. A great-grandmother's name." Danny counted on his fingers. "If she was still alive she'd be about 85."

Tyler stared at the girl's grave. Someone, a long time ago, had planted lilies-of-the-valley by the stone, and although there were quite a few weeds, the lilies dominated. Tyler couldn't imagine Ellen as an old lady. She'd been only fourteen. He couldn't imagine anything killing him. Maybe she had cancer. Or galloping consumption, whatever that was, that people always got in old books.

"This is boring. Let's go."

Danny started walking away, and Tyler followed, relieved that Danny hadn't tried to kick over Ellen's tombstone.

They got on their bikes and headed toward Danny's house. While Tyler was trying not to gasp for breath as he stood on the pedals of his bike to keep up with Danny's pace, Danny coasted in a wide serpentine, swerving only when a car came down the road, slowed for him, then beeped. Danny then made a gesture the driver would only see in their rearview mirror.

Finally they reached a long, wooded driveway full of potholes. Danny jumped off his bike and waited for Tyler to grind to a halt and dismount. "It's better to walk up the driveway. One pothole and bam, you skinned off half your face. Plus my brother, he just got his license, and he likes to play chicken."

Tyler was too winded to comment.

They started walking up the driveway, Danny ahead of Tyler. There was something familiar about Danny, but Tyler couldn't place it. It might have been that Danny was so much like all the boys at the youth correctional center in Lowell where Tyler had lived for a year after the fire incident.

Danny's house was finally coming into sight.

Tyler followed at his own pace, taking note of the yard. No wonder his mother hadn't heard of the Krulls moving in—they'd clearly moved in with someone else. This was no new house with boxes still unpacked. Rusted out cars—some classics from the seventies, Tyler noted, but mostly Buicks and Oldsmobiles and Fords—all with pieces like headlights, wheels, or doors missing, were strewn like carcasses on the lawn. Tricycles, plastic Fisher Price play sets, and sports equipment littered the sparse clumps of grass. Weeds waist high grew against the house.

"I have something to show you. I know you'll really like this." Danny raced ahead and around the corner of his house.

Tyler stepped over the remains of a volleyball net twisted on the ground, sending a slew of grasshoppers leaping out of his path. A doll head looked up at him with one eye stuck open and the other one closed.

Danny was waiting beside a shed that had seen better days. "Come on, you're gonna love this."

Once Tyler was close enough, Danny threw the doors open. He looked like Willy Wonka opening the doors to the Chocolate Factory, only he was wearing a stained sleeveless shirt instead of a purple velvet coat, and a red bandana around his head instead of a top hat.

Tyler squinted into the dark space. Piles of boxes were all he saw.

"What's the big deal?" he asked.

"Look—LOOK!"

Tyler leaned forward to read the labels on the boxes. Magic Carpet, 2000 Beyond, Sky Jacks, Blue-Blinged Willows, Rain Fire, TNT Illuminator, all with the name of a fireworks company stamped on the bottom. His eyes took in the boxes, piled haphazardly on top of one another, and more further back. There had to be hundreds of fireworks in here.

Just one spark, one lit match and the whole place would explode.

"My dad got them real cheap the day after Fourth of July, up in New Hampshire, you know, cuz they're legal there," Danny bragged. "One night you'll have to sleep over so we can do a real show. It's not much fun in the daytime."

"Wow," was all Tyler could think of to say. He was too busy mentally calculating how many explosives were sitting in front of him.

"Okay, okay." Danny shooed him out of the shed and closed the doors. "My dad'll be pissed if he saw us fooling around in here."

Tyler licked his lips. "Can't we light up a few now?"

"My dad will kill me." Danny closed the latch on the shed door, then grabbed Tyler's arm. "Come on. We have a fire pit. Let's go burn some stuff."

An enormous pile of scrap wood and cardboard had hidden the cinderblock fire pit. Danny started chucking in pieces, and once Tyler followed suit, Danny ran to get the lighter fluid and matches.

Tyler stared at the jumble of wood, itching to straighten out the pieces into a standard log cabin or teepee. His family always went camping in the summers, and his father had taught him early on how to position the wood over the kindling and light it with newspapers so you didn't have to use lighter fluid. He'd always liked watching how the fire was born, weak like a baby at first, then accumulating strength. Tyler also liked learning how to blow on the fire, which common sense said would put it out, like a candle flame. Instead, the air was like more fuel.

Of course, after he'd done his time for setting a fire in that dumpster, the family camping trips had stopped.

The smell of gasoline smacked him in the face and woke him up. Danny sprayed it liberally all over the pile of wood, then fumbled with the matches. Tyler regarded him with his arms crossed over his chest.

"So you used to live in Lowell?" Tyler asked.

"Yeah." Danny scraped a match against the side of the box. It lit, but he dropped it on the ground. He stomped it out with his sneaker and pulled out another. "You did too, right?"

"Yeah." Tyler refocused on the waiting wood. "Do you think we went to the same school?"

"I know we did." Danny finally got a match lit and dropped it into the wood. He jumped back a bit in anticipation of the fire, but Tyler knew it would take a couple of seconds. He was far enough away for a fire this small.

The wood ignited instantly, blue flames racing to the limits of where the fluid had hit it. The blaze was momentary, though. With the exception of a few pieces of cardboard and crumpled paper, the fire died down.

Tyler watched the papers burning, the fire struggling to survive. He wanted to ask Danny how he knew Tyler was a pyro, but right now the fire consumed all his attention.

Vaguely he was aware that Danny stood there the same way, staring into the flames.

His mind drifted to the abandoned house. The old wood called to him. He could see it burning almost as clearly as the wood before him now. With fire, the wood would reveal secrets in the hissing of its flesh burning. Secrets of the past and who had once lived there.

From far away he heard Danny ask if he wanted to make s'mores. He nodded, and Danny darted inside. When he returned, he had other people with him. A boy about five years old wearing a Yankees baseball hat and t-shirt, with greasy black hair just like Danny's. A couple of little girls, with skinny limbs sticking out of dirty shorts and tank tops. One looked about eleven, the other about eight. Danny introduced them as his cousins, said their names, but Tyler wasn't listening.

He couldn't tear his eyes away from the fire.

Tyler returned to the present when a bucket of water dampened the flames with a hiss. The sky was purple, growing toward twilight. Tyler blinked and tried to remember where he was.

"I gotta go home for dinner," he told Danny.

"No need. We're cooking up some hot dogs."

Tyler registered the grill and the scents that made his stomach rumble. "I really have to go. My parents will be pissed if I'm not home for dinner."

"All right man." Danny held up one hand and Tyler allowed him to take him through some secret handshake that involved bumping fists and shoulders and snapping. "Later, dude."

Tyler's bike found its way there. Up a back road his father liked to use, to the sign that said, "Hidden Drive." He stopped at the sign, his leg muscles aching.

When he was younger, he had asked his father what "hidden drive" meant. "It means there's a driveway or a road right around the corner, so you need to watch out for people coming out," his dad had answered. After that, Tyler had started looking for a driveway right around the bend, but he'd never seen one. He had figured that it must bc really well hidden.

The sign had fallen down at some point, the post bent and twisted as though a car had hit it and driven off. The yellow was dirty, the words hidden by the brush.

Tyler stashed his bike in the overgrown shrubs by the sign and started walking.

In the brush, just a few paces in from the road, lay the remains of a mailbox, a bent post, the black paint peeling off to reveal rusted metal underneath. Ivy had wrapped itself around the post, and the box itself was full of dead leaves. Once someone had stuck metal letters on the side of the box. All that remained was a crooked B and an SAL.

Birdsall. That's what it spelled. Just like the girl in the cemetery. Just like the labels on the prescription bottles he'd found at the house.

He looked up, where he knew the road led. The pull was strong, but the exhaustion thrumming through his legs was stronger.

He got on his bike and headed home.

Chapter 7

On Monday Tyler sat in suspension, reclining in his chair and trying not to fall asleep. His eyes kept slipping shut. The sun was glaring in from the windows. This first period of doing nothing was killing him. Last week he read that damn manual about three times, and even copied it out once. He didn't bother to write an essay reflecting on what he'd done wrong. So he'd punched Danny. Now they were friends. What was the big deal? Fifty years ago, kids probably fought at school every day. And probably no one got suspended over it, either.

After he'd gotten back from the house last night – having stayed much later than he'd thought - he'd stayed up half the night thinking about the house. He was trying to imagine what it looked like back when people really lived there. This morning he brought his old sketchbook to school with him. There were only five empty pages left, and Tyler had looked through all his old, horrible drawings. Most of them were of cars he'd dreamed up, or robot-car hybrids like Transformers.

Tyler opened to a new page and started drawing. Danny kept looking over his shoulder. The questions Danny wanted to ask seemed to reach Tyler telepathically, carried by Danny's frantic energy: Whatcha drawing? Is that a house? Is that your house? Why are you drawing? Are you taking art classes? Even when Tyler hunched his shoulder over to block Danny's view, Danny still didn't get the hint. Tyler had only drawn a couple of lines before Mr. Edward cut it short. "This isn't art class, Mr. McCracken."

Tyler had gratefully put his sketchbook away, but now he had nothing to do and it was making him tired.

There were quite a few new faces in suspension today. Ben was gone—Tyler had a feeling he'd probably skipped—but Ben's friend Pete Franklin was there. Tyler wished he knew what Pete had done. Mr. Edward had been tight-lipped on the matter, so it must have been really bad, but not bad enough for him to be suspended out of school.

Tyler frowned, thinking of how Mr. Edward had had no problem blabbing Tyler's crime. But then he thought about the house and calmed down.

When the bell rang, Tyler bolted forward. "Good morning, Mr. McCracken," said Mr. Edward, his voice dripping with sarcasm. "Hope we didn't wake you."

Tyler rubbed his eyes, then rested his chin on his fist to wait for Miss Donoghue to show up.

Sure enough, once Mr. Edward had exited, Danny leaned over and said, "What were you drawing?"

"Just a house," Tyler mumbled. He couldn't take out his sketchbook again, not if he wanted to keep the house a secret from Danny.

There was nothing to do but homework. He'd finished reading The House of Seven Gables, so that was done, but there was still a lot of math homework. Science was mostly reading. He wondered how hard it would be to carry his science textbook out to the abandoned house. He supposed he could take his backpack—then he could bring some snacks and supplies with him, too.

"What are you drawing?" Danny asked again.

Tyler had barely realized he was drawing. He looked down to see a girl's face covering the lower half of the page his math homework was on. The eyes looked up at him, familiar and knowing, wispy hair framing the face in soft waves.

"Who's that?" Danny asked.

"Nobody," Tyler said quickly, and slammed his math notebook closed.

"Oh, I get it." Danny said it knowingly, and Tyler wondered what he knew. He probably thought it was some girl he liked. Tyler hauled out his science book and started reading.

***

Tyler started whistling as he threw all of his textbooks into his locker at the end of the day. All his homework was finished. His backpack felt so light, with just his sketchbook and his sweatshirt stuffed in there.

Now he just had to wait around a bit for Danny to get on his bike and head home, so Danny wouldn't see him heading up High Street to the hidden drive. He slipped into the dark cafeteria to the vending machines. Through the big windows overlooking the school's back parking lot, Tyler saw a kid on a bike flying up Proctor Hill. The greasy black hair, the bony arms, the lack of a backpack—Tyler was safe. He tucked his snack into his bag and hurried out of school.

Once he reached the hidden drive, once he'd carefully gotten through the bushes without leaving a trail, he finally felt free enough to run.

The house was exactly as he left it. The kitchen door seemed to be opening much easier now. When he got home to his own house, he still had to worry about taking his shoes off at the door and not leaving his backpack on the stairs, and not eating in his room. Here there was none of that. He could make as much noise as he wanted. He could do whatever he wanted.

Of course, he didn't want to make a lot of noise. He wanted to sit still and listen to the silence. That was one thing missing at his house. There were all kinds of electronic things that made noise even when they weren't on, a kind of a barely audible hum that clogged his mind. And of course cars speeding by, the dog next door barking...

Here, almost nothing. No sounds of civilization, anyway. Just birds outside, wind, the creaking of wood.

Tyler headed upstairs immediately. He lay down on the bed he now thought of as Ellen Birdsall's.

Hours disappeared.

***

"Where have you been?" his mother asked the second he walked through the door.

He nearly jumped out of his skin. He'd been checking his watch; she shouldn't have been home for a few more minutes. How long had she been waiting?

"I was just... walking."

"Not lighting fires out in the woods again, I hope?"

"No!"

After the dumpster incident, and his summer in juvie, he had set a few fires out in the woods. Nobody had gotten hurt, and his parents wouldn't have even known about it if the neighbors hadn't asked why they were burning leaves all the time.

"You weren't hanging out with that Krud boy by any chance, were you?"

His mother was ticked about something, and he had no clue what it was. Normally, he knew exactly why she was mad. It made it a little easier to play dumb.

"His last name is Krull, not Krud. And no, I wasn't hanging out with him today. I went for a hike. That's all."

"Well, I don't think it's a good idea to be hanging around with him." His mother backed off and went back to preparing dinner. "Since you mentioned that he was new in the area, I did a little research. I was correct about his family not buying a new home. They moved in with some relatives of theirs. The Krulls are not the best people."

"What does that mean?" Tyler asked.

"Look, I don't like to judge," his mother started.

Tyler narrowed his eyes. But you will anyway, won't you?

"They live out in that house in the middle of the woods, and hardly anyone has seen your friend's uncle even though he's lived there for years and years. Apparently he lives off welfare handouts and hunting down squirrels. And from what I've heard, that boy is a delinquent. Sharon told me he threatened a teacher on the first day of school?"

Sharon Kingsley was his mother's coworker, and got most of her gossip from her daughter Carolyn, who was in Tyler's grade.

"Yeah, that's what Mr. Edward said." Tyler didn't know why he was adding fuel to her fire. He wished he hadn't said it. Especially when she slammed down a pot and glared at him.

"And you still thought it was okay to spend all day Saturday with this hoodlum?"

Now Tyler was stuck. "I—well, mostly I felt bad, because he was the kid I punched in the face."

It was his mother's turn to be stuck. He'd given her a choice: she could think he was causing trouble with the new thug in town, or she could think he was trying to make up for one bad decision.

Luckily she went with the latter choice. "That's awfully kind of you, Tyler, but really, you don't need to be hanging around with him. He's a bad influence."

Tyler wished he could scream at his mother to stop being a hypocrite. After all, what if Mike's parents had said the same thing about Tyler? He'd been in much worse trouble than Danny back then.

He went upstairs, feeling defeated. Either he was friends with the wrong kind of people, or he was the wrong kind of people.

Chapter 8

Walking into class on Wednesday morning felt strange. The other kids watched him walk in and pause, like they knew he wasn't one of them. Word must have gotten out, since his whole gym class had seen him punch Danny. He had hoped, though, that everyone would have stopped talking about it.

He hesitated to gauge where there were empty seats then selected one near the back, but not the absolute back, because that was where the bad kids sat. He looked around furtively from behind his math textbook.

No one was talking or looking his way. Maybe he was just paranoid.

Then the girl in front of him turned around, swinging a sheaf of honey brown hair over her shoulder.

"Hi, I'm Karin," she said. "What's your name?"

He managed to unstick his mouth. "Tyler."

Karin flashed a perfect smile. Tyler didn't know anyone in this class, so he didn't understand why Karin was talking to him, unless the others elected her as the best candidate to get him to tell her about his sordid past. It would work, too. She was so pretty he was struggling to breathe normally.

"My family just got back from vacation in Hawaii," Karin said. "So I missed the first week of classes."

So that explained her tanned skin. Her beautiful, smooth, golden skin. She raised her eyebrows, and he shut his mouth, which he had suddenly realized was gaping.

"I was hoping you could fill me in?"

His brain finally started working again. She was talking to him because he had his textbook open. She thought he was smart.

Tyler fumbled through his books for his notebook and started flipping through the pages. "Sure." He hoped she couldn't tell that there weren't any notes from class, only the homework he'd done in suspension. "Uh, it's mostly been review, you know, quadratic equations and stuff. This was our homework—"

He suddenly stopped flipping pages. Ellen's face gazed out at him from the bottom of the page. In a panic, he started to tear the page out, but Karin's hand stopped him. She was touching him.

"You're a really good artist," Karin said, turning the notebook so she could see the sketch right side up.

"Thanks."

"Who is she?"

His face felt like it was on fire. "I made her up," Tyler said. It suddenly struck him that his picture of Ellen looked a lot like Karin. His stomach clenched with the thought that Karin might think Tyler was obsessed with her, like a stalker, even though he'd only just met her today.

"You're a really good artist," Karin repeated, and flashed that perfect smile again.

When she turned back around, that hair poured down her back, and Tyler could barely focus on anything the teacher said all period.

***

It felt good to be able to leave the classroom when the bell rang. Tyler smiled stupidly at Karin, forgetting even to say something intelligent like, "Bye."

Mike Beaumont joined up with him and they headed to English class. "I hope you've been reading House of Seven Gables," Mike said. "Mrs. Tanner likes everyone to participate in discussions."

It took Tyler a second to focus on something else other than Karin Grady. "Yeah, I've been reading it." Tyler didn't breathe a word about having finished it. No need to look like a geek next to a geek.

"I heard you didn't make track. That really sucks. Maybe next year."

"Yeah."

"I'm planning on trying out for basketball. You interested?"

In the crowded hallway, a loud voice started calling his name. "Tyler! Hey, man!"

Tyler's face got hot. He sped up a bit and tried to get to his classroom before Danny caught up to him.

"Is someone calling you?" Mike slowed down, looked over his shoulder.

"No, no, it's fine," Tyler said, trying to edge past some girls talking in the doorway.

"Ty! Wait up!" And suddenly Danny was right there. "Hey! Didn't you hear me calling you?"

"No," Tyler lied.

"Who's this?" Mike asked, looking at Danny like some strange bug.

"No one," Tyler said automatically. "I mean, this is Danny. Danny, this is my friend Mike."

Mike dutifully stuck his hand out, which Danny ignored.

"Nah, you don't look like a Mike." Danny looked Mike up and down. "You look like a Frank. I'm going to call you Frank."

The girls in the doorway overheard and giggled. "Hey, Frank."

"What's going on, Danny," Tyler asked, before Mike could ask any questions.

"Not much. What lunch do you have? Since we're not in any of the same classes except gym. I didn't know you were one of the smart kids."

The hall was starting to clear out. The girls headed in to their seats and Mike followed.

"I have first lunch." Tyler edged into the classroom.

Danny edged forward with him. "Me too. Are you in advanced Algebra? Cuz maybe you can help me out after school. I'm totally lost."

The bell rang. Tyler kept backing up, but soon Danny was inside the classroom too. "Sure, whatever. Aren't you going to be late?"

"It's no big deal."

It was a big deal to Mrs. Tanner. She stood at the front of the classroom, hands on her hips, staring at Danny and Tyler with raised eyebrows. "Excuse me, are either of you boys in this class?"

"I am," Tyler said quickly and took his seat. Mrs. Tanner turned to Danny.

"Not me. I'm just visiting." He flashed the teacher a grin.

Mrs. Tanner did not smile back.

"Well, gotta go. See ya, Ty."

Tyler wished he could crawl under his desk. Especially when Mrs. Tanner returned to him, her eyes huge behind thick glasses. "And what is your name?"

He cleared his throat. His face was on fire. "Tyler McCracken."

Mrs. Tanner made a note in her grade book. "Next time, Tyler, leave your conversations in the hallway."

Luckily Tyler was able to make up for his bad second first impression during the book discussion. No one except Tyler and a couple other kids had much to say, which Mrs. Tanner interpreted as no one having read the assigned chapters.

Toward the end of the period, Mrs. Tanner announced an assignment. "Rather than doing a book report, I'd like all of you to do a research report on an historical house or building," she explained. Several students groaned, and a smattering of conversations popped up about being overloaded with work.

Tyler looked at the assignment sheet. "I'd like you to choose a local house with some history. It could be your own house, or one of the houses in the historical district, as long as you are able to find enough information about the house to fill two to three pages. There are plenty of resources at the library."

"That's impossible!" said a girl at the back of the classroom. "What kind of stuff are we going to find out about a house? And what does this have to do with English class?"

"Writing research papers is something you have to learn in English class, Carolyn," Mrs. Tanner said. "And we are essentially reading about the history of a house right now, are we not?"

A few more students complained, but Tyler already knew what house he was going to do his report on.

Chapter 9

Dinner was an elaborate affair that night. Candles on the table, steaks. Tyler's mother was humming, along with the radio. "To what do we owe this honor?" his dad asked.

"Sam called me at work today," his mother answered.

Of course, Tyler thought darkly. Anything for his sister, even when she wasn't there.

"She said she's coming home Columbus Day weekend." She put the plate of juicy medium rare steaks on the table. "She's got a lot of work, so she can't get away until then, but she thinks she'll do well in all of her classes, and she's made a lot of new friends."

Tyler's mom babbled on and on about Sam for most of dinner, which allowed Tyler to eat faster than usual. Before he went up to his bedroom, he asked his mom if she could pick him up at the library tomorrow on her way home from work.

"The library? What do you need to do there?" she asked.

"I have a research paper."

"Great! That's no problem, I'll swing by around five."

Things were so much better when his mom was in a good mood. Someday, Tyler thought, it'd be nice if he was the one to cause the good mood.

***

The Middlebury Public Library was much smaller than Tyler expected. Inside the intimidating brick exterior, shelves reached far over his head, crammed with books. He walked up to the librarian at the reference desk and hesitantly explained what he needed.

"You'll be able to find everything you need down in the History Room," she said, and led him down a steep flight of stairs to a door that was barred and locked like a jail cell. The librarian had the key on a big key ring.

The History Room was small but packed with old newspapers and maps and books that had probably been sitting there for centuries. The librarian indicated a metal box with a drawer. "This is an index of houses in town listed by their street address, and it'll tell you where to find information about previous owners. This map up here also has each house labeled by owner, circa 1850."

Tyler looked up at the yellowed map, frozen behind a dusty layer of glass.

"These books here are all about town history, so once you find the owners, you might be able to find out some information about them. We also have a computer down here—" The librarian paused to remove a dust cover from a machine straight out of the early nineties. "It's slow, but you can search the databases for newspaper articles going back to 1802. And there's always microfilm. Are you all set?"

Tyler looked around and took a deep breath and nodded.

He had no idea what street the house was even on, or if it had been around long enough to fit Mrs. Tanner's qualifications for a "historical house."

At first he couldn't even find his own road on the historical map. Then, after looking around, he found a recent map of Middlebury. It turned out his road hadn't existed in 1850. The hidden drive also wasn't listed on the modern map, probably because it was a driveway, not a road. He stared at the historical map, trying to orient the hidden drive with the other roads he knew. The closest he could find was a thin line denoted as "Logging Road." He returned to the modern map, and found the name of the road the hidden drive intersected with: Pine Hill Road. The modern map didn't have little squares marking land ownership, but there were tiny numbers. Tyler, thinking these were house numbers, examined the numbers corresponding to the position of the "Logging Road." He figured the number of the abandoned house must be between 50 and 65 Pine Hill Road.

He looked carefully at all the index cards labeled with those street addresses. All of them had present owners within the past twenty years. The abandoned house had been vacant for much longer than that, he was sure.

He was about to give up when he remembered the computer. He hit the power button and waited for it to boot up. When he finally got to the search screen, his fingers hesitated over the keyboard as he tried to decide whether he should look up "Logging Road" or "Pine Hill Road." He had a sudden idea. He typed out, "Ellen Birdsall."

Several minutes later, three results popped up on the screen.

"Ellen Birdsall, age 14" was the title of the first, listed as part of the Obituaries section of the November 14, 1936 edition of the Middlebury Post. Tyler clicked on the link.

"Ellen Miriam Birdsall, aged fourteen years, passed away on November 8. She is survived by her parents, Theodore and Belinda Birdsall of Birdsall Drive. Funeral services will be private."

Birdsall Drive! Could this be the hidden road Tyler had found? Maybe. Tyler returned to the index. No card for Birdsall Drive. Tyler returned to the computer and sat back in the chair, disappointed at the article's brevity. Nothing about how she died at all. All he'd found was a possibility.

He hit the back button and looked at the other two articles. One was an announcement of the marriage of Ellen's parents, dated 1918. The other was much more interesting:

"Girl Found Wandering in Forest Claims to be Ellen Birdsall"—dated 1971.

Eagerly, Tyler clicked on the link.

Immediately the computer screen went black, the hum of the computer's CPU silent. Tyler removed his hand from the mouse and backed up the chair. "What the heck?" he muttered. He pushed the power button. Nothing happened. He checked the plug. It was still in the wall.

He slowly clenched and unclenched his fists, trying to avoid punching out the monitor.

"Stupid piece of junk," he muttered.

He stepped over to the wall of historical books. The books were useless without the index cards, but Tyler browsed the titles anyway. Like there would be some book all about the Birdsall family.

Most of the books had titles like A Brief History of Middlebury, Massachusetts, or Early Settlers of Middlebury Village. Tyler picked a few at random and checked the indexes for mentions of anyone or any street named Birdsall, or Logging Road. Nothing, no surprise there. Then Tyler's eyes happened on a book called Local Ghost Stories and Legends of Middlesex County. He pulled it out and sat back down in the chair, with the black eye of the computer monitor watching him.

The largest sections of the book dealt with the cities like Lowell, Cambridge, and Natick. There was a short chapter devoted to the towns of Middlebury, Renford, and Oakridge.

Tyler lost himself reading about how the private Catholic school in Oakridge had its own ghost of a former nun whose upper half had been sighted by several students, and how an inn originally built as a mansion in the late 1700s was plagued by a playful spirit that enjoyed rearranging the silverware in the dining room. Renford residents had sighted the ghost of a man standing in the center of the gazebo on the town common with a noose around his neck, who would seem to drop through the gazebo floor then disappear. The book's author reported that the man was the ghost of Wilton Crow, who had been sentenced to hang for the axe murder of his family back in the days of the Puritans, and the gazebo had been built on the site of the gallows where he was hanged.

The only ghost story taking place in Middlebury had to do with some young girls in the early 1700s seeing apparitions in the forest. At first the townspeople had dismissed what the girls said, because they were wary of another Salem witch hunt. When the girls began acting strangely, a group of men went up to where the girls claimed to have seen the ghosts, and found a mysterious circle of stones. They believed the circle had been made by witches, and the stones were moved out of the circle formation to break their power. The girls soon recovered, but no one had been accused of witchcraft.

A noise in the doorway caught him off guard. His back spasmed bolt upright and the book fell to the floor.

"Tyler?"

It was only his mother.

"I've been waiting outside. I thought you were going to come out at five."

"Sorry, I was just reading this book." Tyler picked the book up off the floor, relieved that he hadn't damaged it. The book wasn't too old anyway, published in the 1950s. It seemed to have been written based mostly on rumors instead of real research anyway. "It's all about ghosts."

"I thought you were here to do a school report," his mother said.

"Yeah, I was, but I saw this and it looked interesting. I'm not having much luck finding stuff about the house..." Tyler stopped himself from saying, "The house I found." He finished with, "The house I'm doing my report on."

"You have to do a report on a house? Why didn't you say so? You could have come down to the office. We have all kinds of records there. Does it have to be a haunted house?"

"No, it just has to be historical."

"What house did you have in mind? Our house has some good history."

Tyler put all his stuff in his backpack and put the dust cover back on the broken computer, trying to avoid the question, or give himself some time to think of a good lie. "Um... there's this house up on Pine Hill Road? You know that one with the stone wall?"

He congratulated himself silently. It was an impressive looking house, a mansion practically, but it was far too new.

"Ah, the Duvalls' house. That was built in the nineteen-twenties, I think. You couldn't find anything? I've heard the Duvalls were a big deal for the town. They practically owned Middlebury back in the day."

"Oh. I thought the house was older. I think Mrs. Tanner wants us to pick houses that are at least a century old."

"I can put together some of the information I have about our own house for your report," his mother offered. They headed out to the car, Tyler's mom babbling about how their house had been built in the 1850s and how she suspected that the room in the basement now occupied by the furnace had been used in the Underground Railroad.

Tyler nodded absently. He wanted to ask why there would need to be a secret room when slaves were free in the north. He suspected that the room in the basement might have been a slave or servant's bedroom, if it wasn't a pantry or something.

After dinner, Tyler got on his home computer and went to the library's webpage. He found the newspaper database and again typed in the search, "Ellen Birdsall." He clicked on the third link.

The page hadn't yet loaded when his phone rang, making him jump. He looked at the screen: Danny. He groaned, then answered. "Hey."

"Hey! Tyler!"

Tyler wiggled the mouse, wishing the page would load faster. "What's up."

"Not much. You wanna hang out tomorrow night?"

"What do you want to do?"

"My parents aren't going to be home, and my brother's having some friends over. I want to watch a marathon of the Saw movies. My brother got the box set."

"Um... I'll have to check with my parents."

"Just tell them my big brother will be there. Or you could lie and say my parents will be there. Whatever. Your parents are strict, huh?"

Tyler stared at the circle symbol that meant the page was still loading. It kept rotating, but nothing was happening. "They're not too bad," he said.

"My parents pretty much lets me do whatever I want," Danny said. "I mean, they get pissed when the school calls home and stuff, but they don't really care what I do as long as I don't get in trouble."

And Tyler tended to get upset when his parents didn't get pissed. "I don't know, my parents are okay. Hey, I have some homework to do. I'll let you know tomorrow at school what they say." He already knew they wouldn't say yes. Especially not his mom.

"Sure, man."

Tyler hung up the phone and looked back at the screen. The page had loaded—but it was the standard, "This page is not available" error page. Tyler clicked back and tried the link again. Same message.

Frustrated, he poked the off button on the monitor and went out to the living room. "Hey, can I hang out over at Danny's tomorrow night?" he asked.

"Sure," his father said automatically.

"Danny who?" his mother asked, giving his father an icy stare.

"You know, that kid Danny Krull? He asked me to hang out. He said his older brother will be there."

"How old is this brother?"

"I don't know. He has his driver's license."

Tyler's mother looked at his father steadily for a long time. Finally she looked at Tyler. "I don't think this is a good idea."

"Come on, we're just going to be watching movies." Tyler had to stop himself. What was he doing? Reading a script?

"I told you, I don't want you hanging around with that boy," his mother said sharply. Then she softened. "Even if you are just trying to be nice."

Tyler sighed, and tried to sound as annoyed as possible. "Fine."

Danny took the news better than Tyler had expected. "That's fine, man. You gotta obey the 'rents." A tall upperclassman with Danny's greasy black hair walked by and slapped Danny on the shoulder. "See you later, Ty."

"Yeah, see you," Tyler said, relieved. He'd been lucky that Danny had taken to sitting at lunch with his older brother and his brother's friends. It left him free to sit with Mike... and Karin. She and a couple of her friends had begun sitting near Tyler and his friends at lunch, because Gretchen liked Mike, at least according to Karin. She had confided this to Tyler during math class one day, although Tyler hadn't seen Gretchen speak to Mike once, or even sit near him. Karin, on the other hand, sat right next to Tyler and prodded him into conversation every day.

He didn't know why Karin seemed to like him, but she did, and it made Tyler the envy of his lunch table. He only wished he could do more than blush and speak in monosyllables when she was around.

Chapter 10

Weeks slid by. Tyler spent as much time as he could out at the house. Most days he spent on Ellen's bed, reading, either things for school or when he ran out of school work, books he found at the library that he never would have considered reading before. Authors like Louisa May Alcott or Charles Dickens or Jane Austen. He checked these books out at the library under the guise of a book report, and kept the books hidden at the bottom of his backpack, or in one of the drawers in Ellen's vanity. He liked leaving a little part of himself at the house, even if the library books weren't technically his.

Usually he was able to make it home before his parents, and he wouldn't have to lie about where he'd been. If they ever asked, he said he'd gone for a run or a hike. He told them that even though he hadn't made the track team, he wanted to train for cross-country.

Sometimes he didn't even think he was lying.

Danny kept trying to get him to hang out, but so far Tyler's excuse that his parents wouldn't let him had held up. He felt bad when he saw Danny at lunch – Danny sat with his older brothers who made fun of him, and Danny took the abuse because he thought it was cool to hang out with older kids, and also because he hadn't made any other friends.

Tyler was starting to look forward to his sister coming home for Columbus Day weekend, his birthday weekend. The way his parents worshipped her annoyed him, but Sam was fun to hang around with. Sam being home made his birthday feel more special.

The end of September also meant Homecoming Weekend.

"Are you going to the football game tonight?" Karin asked that Friday in math class. She twisted a piece of her sunlight-colored hair around her finger.

"Yeah," Tyler said, even though he hadn't been planning on it. His dad liked football; he could probably convince his dad to bring him. "Why?"

"Well, you know I'm a cheerleader." She gave him a shy, sweet smile. "And during third quarter we have a break. Maybe you'd want to hang out with me?"

How could Tyler say no with those gray eyes pleading with him?

"I mean," Karin dropped her voice and leaned in closer. Tyler could smell her hair, an old-fashioned flowery scent. "I'm not really friends with the other cheerleaders. My mom made me join the squad."

"Then you will definitely see me at the game," Tyler said. "I'm not a huge football fan, but my dad likes it. I wanted to join the track team—"

Tyler practically smacked himself for even mentioning it.

"Why didn't you?"

Tyler exhaled. "I tried out, but I didn't make it." He hoped Karin hadn't heard about Tyler punching Danny. If Karin's parents were as strict as she made them sound, they'd be giving her the "he's a bad influence" speech.

"That's too bad."

Now she'd only think he was some loser who didn't make the team because he wasn't a good runner.

"I'm training really hard," he said quickly. "I'm thinking of trying out for cross-country so I've been running up hills in the woods and stuff." God, he sounded stupid. And he was just feeding her the same lie he fed his parents.

"Cool! I would love to do some running. I get out of shape when it's not soccer season." Karin? Out of shape? Tyler only had to look at her smooth tan legs to see that could never happen. "Maybe we could run together sometime. It's always good to train with some competition."

How could he not fall in love with this girl?

After school, Tyler ran up the hill to the abandoned house. The kitchen looked better now, after he'd brought a trash bag and swept out all the leaves and litter a couple of weeks ago. Today he went into the office and sorted through some of the papers in there. He'd been hoping to find something about the house's history. All he needed was one envelope that proved that the road outside was called Birdsall Drive. Most of the scraps of paper looked like legal documents, but Tyler couldn't find any names. A lot of the papers on the floor were torn up too, and it was hard to find any cohesiveness among the scraps. He read on one piece, "the basement appears to be the source of," while another read, "in the event of an emergency" and another, "The stones are."

Nothing made sense. He threw the scraps of paper on the floor in frustration.

Suddenly, the frustration he'd been feeling since school started crashed down on him. He grabbed up bits of paper and twisted them, tearing them into little pieces. "Stupid, stupid," he muttered. "I'm not even smart enough to find a damn house!"

He punched the top of the desk, and was rewarded when the old dry wood splintered. "Can't do anything right, can't even be friends with the right people!" He kicked the side of the desk. A loud crack seemed to echo through the house.

He could feel himself losing control. His shaking hands picked up more paper and ripped it—but instead of throwing it on the floor, he made a little pile on the desk. He stared at it.

What am I doing?

His hands knew what he was doing. Out of his pocket came the little orange lighter he kept hidden.

What am I doing?

His fingers were shaking so much he couldn't get the rusty wheel to turn. The dry clicks of the flint made the trembling stop. And then, the little flame.

He stared at it, his thumb growing hot. Could anything be so beautiful?

The tiny fire nibbled at the old paper, then caught ravenously. Tyler knelt right beside it, encouraging it with little puffs of air. His mind wrapped around the fire until it became his everything.

Upstairs, door hinges creaked open.

Tyler froze, his mind suddenly away from the fire. That could have been anything—maybe a gust of wind had blown one of the doors open.

Except he always made sure the doors were shut before he left. He'd never gone back into the rooms he called the parents' bedroom and the black hole room; those doors were always shut. What about Ellen's bedroom door? Had he shut it tight behind him yesterday? He'd thought he had.

Abruptly he returned to the fire. What was he thinking, setting a fire in a place like this? The house would go up in about two seconds. It was nothing like that warehouse, made of brick, in the middle of a busy city where any number of people could have set it. No, this fire would be blamed directly on him. Tyler was pretty sure he was the only pyromaniac in tiny little Middlebury.

He jumped up on the desk and stomped out the fire with his sneakers. He stood on the desk, staring down at the smoldering heap of paper, the black burn marks marring the desk's surface. This was the first fire he'd set in years. He'd tried so hard to be good, but always he did stupid stuff.

Because I'm bad. He might as well give up trying to be good.

Then he heard creaks, like footsteps, overhead, and all self-pitying came to a halt. Those footsteps were directly above him. Something had moved from the corner of the office's ceiling to immediately over Tyler's head. He lifted his head and looked up. Ellen's room wasn't over the office, it was over the living room.

His heart thumped loudly in his ears, making it harder to hear. Wind blowing through the house brought whispers. Every hair on his body stood on end.

He didn't want to go upstairs. His feet turned in that direction anyway. He didn't want to go. He had to go. Something pulled at him; he was terrified. His mind went blank as his feet lifted heavily onto each stair, bringing him closer to the thing waiting for him up there.

The hallway was dark except for that beam of sunlight piercing the roof. He couldn't see anything beyond the sun. His feet ascended higher and higher. His fists were clenched at his side, the fingernails digging into his palms.

The door to the tiny bedroom was open. He could tell from the glint of the doorknob in the sunlight. Beyond that patch of sunlight, something moved. A black shadow. The light was too bright to see the darkness. One more step. Another. Something glowed dully in the light, rounded shapes.

The tops of a pair of black shoes.

No supernatural force could make Tyler move another inch. He couldn't breathe. He blinked, but the shoes were still there.

And then they stepped back. Disappeared into the absolute darkness.

He couldn't see anything now. Nothing was there, nothing seemed to be there.

The wind picked up, pushed at the house with such a force pieces of the shingles snapped off. Leaves and branches showered in through the hole. The sunshine disappeared as clouds whipped in front of the sun outside.

The spell now broken, he reversed down the stairs, unwilling to turn his back, tripping several times, which might have caused him to fall if he hadn't been gripping the banister so tightly he would later find deep slivers embedded in his palms.

When he got to the bottom of the stairs, he ran.

He ran out of the house, out to the road, and continued up the road, cutting through the weeds, slipping on loose chunks of rock. He wasn't sure where he was going, all he knew was that he had to get away from that inky black shape that was there but wasn't there but he knew it was there, it had been.

He only stopped when he was exhausted. He flopped onto the ground beside a tree stump and gasped for air. His whole body was shaking—he knew it was adrenaline, but he shivered anyway. Once he'd caught his breath, he realized that there wasn't a hint of wind in the cloudless sky.

He was so amazed by the weather that he'd barely stopped to notice where he was.

There were no live trees within fifty feet. He was surrounded by tree stumps and waist high grass. He turned and looked further up the hill. More stumps. He must be on that logging road he'd seen on the map.

He moved to sit on a stump. Sweat was pouring down his face and neck. Rubbing at it with one sleeve of his shirt, he gazed around. This was a dead forest. Yet there was something about it that seemed alive.

The logging road was on the 1850 map. How long ago had the logging operation stopped mining these hills? Trees cut down that long ago would have rotted stumps by now. Other trees would have grown up around the stumps, too. There was nothing but weeds here.

He stood up to walk back home. Then he remembered his backpack. It was back there, at the house. He had to go back and get it.

In the glaring sunshine, he didn't feel quite so freaked out. He'd probably imagined the whole thing. That seemed like the most likely explanation.

By the time he got back to the house, he was certain he had imagined it all. All the same, he darted inside the house only long enough to snag his backpack from the kitchen, then got the hell out of there.

Chapter 11

That night at the football game, Tyler sat next to his dad and watched Karin do her cheerleading routines. Once she found him in the bleachers, she waved one pompom at him. Several times throughout the night he thought she looked at him and smiled. He always blushed and tried to focus on the game. His dad kept jumping up and yelling, and Tyler never knew what was going on.

"You okay?" his dad said after the Middlebury team scored a touchdown and Tyler hadn't moved.

"Yeah, I'm fine," Tyler said. "Why?"

"You don't seem to be enjoying yourself. You wanted to come, didn't you?"

"Yeah, yeah. I'm having a good time."

Then his dad noticed that Tyler was watching the cheerleaders. "Oh, I see."

Tyler blushed again, his face burning against the crisp night air.

While his father went for popcorn and sodas at halftime, Tyler stayed to watch the halftime show. Karin was so perfect. A group of kids in Tyler's grade walked by on the bleachers, and Mike Beaumont separated from them and called out to him. "Hey, Tyler! I didn't know you were coming to the game."

"Yeah," Tyler said. "Karin invited me."

"Nice," Mike said. "You going to the Homecoming Dance with her after?"

Tyler swallowed. "I don't know."

"Come on, the rest of us are going."

"Yeah, I just have to talk to Karin about it."

The football players started piling back onto the field. Tyler headed to the front of the bleachers to meet Karin. Her face was flushed, and wisps from her ponytail framed her face like a halo. "Hi," he said.

"Hi," she said.

"Um, you looked good out there."

"Thanks."

"So, uh, are you going to the dance later?"

Karin's face immediately fell. "No. My parents won't let me go to any dances. Not until I'm sixteen."

"Oh," said Tyler awkwardly. "That sucks."

"Yeah. Everyone's going to go and have a good time without me."

"I wasn't planning on going," Tyler offered. "I mean, Mike just told me about it. I figured since you were a cheerleader you were going."

"You're really not going?"

"Not if you're not going."

Her perfect smile was back, beaming at him. "Thanks, Tyler."

They stood on the bleachers and watched the game. Karin had her arms crossed and seemed cold, and she leaned against him for body heat. Third quarter didn't seem to last long enough. All too soon Karin was called back to the cheerleaders.

Tyler was about to head back to where his dad was sitting when he heard someone call his name. He looked around and didn't see anybody he knew.

"Ty! Down here!"

He looked down to see Danny's face under the bleachers.

Underneath the bleachers was a different world. The darkness was only broken apart by slats of light seeping in from the bright world above. He could smell more than see kids smoking, and couples stood entwined in the darker corners. Danny grabbed Tyler by the arm and pulled him toward a group of guys who were smoking. Tyler could see Danny's brothers, and Ben Simms, and some girl wearing too much makeup and Ben's jacket, but he didn't know any of the other people.

"I saw you making your moves on that cheerleader," Danny said. "Nice."

"Thanks," Tyler mumbled.

"You're not going to that stupid dance tonight are you?"

"I wasn't planning on it. Karin's parents won't let her."

"Good. Cuz you're coming with us."

Tyler didn't say anything. What could he say? "What am I supposed to tell my dad?"

"Tell him you're going to the dance with that chick, and that her parents will give you ride home. Then, when he leaves, you come to my house. My parents are home, it's not like it's a big deal. But you keep backing out on me, man. I'm beginning to think you don't like me." Danny made a pretend pouty face.

Ben laughed meanly.

"I mean, you can't still be grounded over the whole fight thing, can you?"

Tyler wondered if that was what Danny had told everyone, that they'd gotten into a fight. When really it had been one-sided: Tyler punching Danny, and Danny going down like a sack of bricks.

"No," Tyler said. "Let me go tell my dad." He walked up to the bleachers like a man going to fill his death sentence.

***

Tyler stood nervously a safe distance away from the gymnasium door – close enough to look like he was going in and waiting for Karin, far enough that Mike and the other guys might not see him and assume he was going to the dance. He watched his dad walk out to the car, and waved as he drove away, feeling abandoned even though he was the one who had lied to his dad. Because he was still technically grounded, he didn't have his cell phone or any way to call his dad for a ride, no way to escape the party at Danny's house except on foot.

When the taillights of his father's car disappeared out of the parking lot, he headed toward Danny's brother's car.

He didn't know what he was doing. He should have lied to Danny and not his father. He didn't want to go to this party or hang out with Danny. But he felt like he had to go, to play out the role of the juvenile delinquent, the pyromaniac.

Danny's brother Max, a taller, more muscular version of Danny, revved the engine of his black Mustang impatiently. Danny yelled through the open window, "Come on Tyler, let's go!"

In the tiny backseat of the Mustang, Tyler was crammed tight against Danny's side. One of Max's friends shared the back with them. He was smoking a cigarette, and the open windows made the smoke whip around into Tyler's face. The friend in the front passenger seat turned on the music, cranked it so high Tyler felt like the drum was beating against his brain.

Max laid some rubber when he peeled out of the school parking lot up Proctor Hill.

"Slow it down, man, you don't want the cops to pull you over," said Max's friend, his voice barely audible over the music. Max slowed down marginally, then sped back up when he got to the deserted back roads.

The lights were ablaze at the Krull's house. Tyler could see sparks spraying across the backyard. Danny punched the back of Max's seat. "Yeah! Fireworks!"

Tyler's stomach fluttered.

They tumbled out of the vehicle when it skidded to a rough stop. Tyler followed Danny out to the backyard, not quite running like Danny was, but walking faster. A blaze shot up into the sky with a whistle, then BANG! It sounded like a gunshot, with fiery droplets bright against the night sky.

"Woo hoo!" Danny yelled, pumping a fist in the air.

About twenty or thirty people milled around the backyard, gathering around the roaring inferno in the fire pit. Most of them had bottles or cans in their hands.

"Hey, does your friend want a beer?" Max asked Danny, opening a cooler.

"Yeah," Danny answered for Tyler. Tyler accepted the ice cold can, almost relieved that he didn't have to do the whole "I'm not allowed to drink" thing. What could one drink hurt?

Danny and Tyler moved closer to the bonfire and sat down on the grass to watch the fireworks. Tyler watched the older boys dancing around with a torch, touching the flame to the fuses and sending them off into the sky. It was a never-ending cycle of fire.

Danny couldn't sit still as long as Tyler; he kept jumping up to get refills on the alcohol. Tyler got lost in watching the explosions in the sky. The next time he looked down at the drink in his hand, there were three other cans on the ground beside him. Danny was gone.

Tyler got up, fell down, got back up. He could see Danny near the launch site and stumbled toward his friend. No one seemed to notice him weaving all over the lawn. "Hey Danny," Tyler said. His voice sounded too low. "Let's light up a few."

"That's what I'm trying to tell Max," Danny said, rolling his eyes. "He doesn't want to listen to me."

"Lemme talk to him," Tyler said. He shoved Danny out of the way, almost falling over himself, and walked up to Max. "Hey. Let me light off a few."

Max looked at Tyler and grinned. "Hey guys, the nerd here is drunk," he said to his friends, who laughed.

Tyler's face burned with embarrassment and drunkenness. "Come on." He lunged for the torch.

"No way, kid," Max said. "You are wasted."

Danny came over and grabbed Tyler, dragged him over to the fire. "What's your brother's problem," Tyler complained. "I just wanna set a couple off."

"Don't worry about it," Danny said.

They stared at the fire for a while.

"So what have you been up to lately, man?" Danny asked. "I hardly ever see you. And you're never at home after school."

The words slipped out of Tyler's mouth before he knew it. "That's because I found this house out in the woods." Oh, crap, he thought.

"A house?"

"Yeah. It's abandoned." Tyler suddenly thought of the best way to keep Danny out of there. He leaned in close to Danny's ear and whispered, "I think it's haunted."

"Really? Cool! Where is it? Let's go!"

Danny was off and running.

Tyler groaned. He should've known better.

"It's really far. We don't even have a flashlight."

Danny didn't want to hear any excuses. "We can ask my brother for a ride. And I'm sure we have some flashlights inside."

"No, no, don't tell your brother," Tyler said. Begged, practically.

"Come on, we need a ride," Danny said, and ignored Tyler's further pleas. "Max! Tyler knows where there's an abandoned house!" he yelled across the backyard.

"An abandoned house?"

"He says it's haunted!"

"Awesome! Let's go!"

Tyler felt sick.

—

Chapter 12

Danny ran inside to grab some flashlights. A fistful of glow sticks appeared out of nowhere. Tyler found himself in the passenger seat of Max's Mustang giving directions. "Turn left here. Okay, stop. We have to walk from here."

There was a group of about eight people, in two cars, stumbling into the woods. Tyler wanted to throw up. He wished there was some way to take this back. The house would never belong to him alone ever again.

Tyler had walked this road almost every day for the past month, but everything looked radically different in the darkness. Ahead of him, flashlight beams bounced along the road, held by running teenagers. He ran only to keep up with the light bearers—he certainly didn't want to be left alone in the dark, not after what he thought he'd seen this afternoon. He'd explained away most of it... but the dark brought it back in full glory.

Those shoes, waiting for him.

They got to the house, stopping to take in the decrepit exterior. "Woooo..." Max moaned, dangling his hands in a girl's face. "I'm the ghost, and I'm coming to get you!"

"Stop it!" she giggled, shoving him away.

Max and his two friends shouldered open the kitchen door. Tyler cringed at the pop of the hinges, the painful squeal of wood splintering. He could see the flashlight beams entering the living room through the window panes; he shuffled through the kitchen door at the back of the group.

He waited in the living room while everyone else explored his house, laid their hands on walls and doorknobs that belonged to him. They trooped upstairs, oblivious to the fact that he had remained behind. He heard them opening the doors, jumping on beds. How hadn't they felt that horrible pull from that dark little room? Tyler found that he was holding his breath, waiting for something to happen.

"This place is so cool," Max was saying. They were coming downstairs now. "These people just up and left all this stuff here? Someone totally got murdered. That's the only explanation."

Danny followed close behind his brother, grinning maniacally. "Hey, let's check out the basement!" he said. "Tyler, do you know where the basement is?"

Tyler shook his head.

"What about that door in the kitchen?" Danny ran around the corner.

Now Tyler realized there was another door in the kitchen, what he'd assumed to be a cabinet. Of course, that would be the basement.

"Max, give me a flashlight!"

The group of kids passed right by Tyler and crowded around Danny.

"I'm not giving you a flashlight, loser. You're too jumpy. Here, I'll hold it so you can see the stairs. I'll be right behind you."

Tyler closed his eyes, knowing what was coming.

The basement door slammed, and Danny screamed. "Hey!"

The other kids laughed.

"Hey! Hey! Let me out!" Danny's fists pounded against the door. The whole house shook with each slam.

"Go find us some ghosts, Danny boy," Max said.

"Come on guys, this isn't funny." There was a tremble in Danny's voice. Tyler found that his jaw had clenched tight, and his fists, too.

"You wanted to see ghosts, right?"

It was clear from the way most of the kids were laughing that they all thought Danny was annoying. They all thought Danny deserved to be in the basement, the dark basement of some deserted old house that might be haunted. They thought it was hilarious.

Their laughter slowly faded behind Tyler's white-hot anger.

"Get out!" he screamed at them suddenly. "Get out!" He stormed at the kids blocking the doorway between the kitchen and the living room.

"What the hell?" The kids tried to shove him off, thinking he was only playing, but Tyler wasn't fooling around. He punched everything in his way, including the doorway, which buckled under his fist.

"Jesus Christ," said one of the guys. He pushed his girlfriend out of the house ahead him. "What a freak."

"Get out of my house!" Tyler screamed.

Everyone except Max headed out the door.

"Chill out, kid. It was just a joke." He pulled at the door, but it seemed stuck. "I was going to let him out in a couple of minutes. See?" Max grabbed the doorknob with both hands. It didn't budge.

Suddenly Danny started screaming and banging against the door. "Let me out! Max! Please! Let me out of here!"

Those were the only words Tyler could understand before Danny descended into unintelligibility.

"Let him out!" Tyler yelled at Max.

"I can't! It's stuck!" Max yanked at the door.

There was a loud clatter, accompanied by silence from Danny.

Max and Tyler stopped and listened. It sounded like Danny had fallen down the stairs.

After several long moments of silence, Max asked, "Danny? Are you okay?"

No answer.

Overhead a door creaked open, and footsteps slowly walked across the ceiling.

"Shit, what was that?" Max whispered.

Tyler knew what it was. This time, the footsteps didn't stop over his head. He could hear them creaking into the hallway. He had to get out of there. He had to get Danny out first.

He pulled at the basement door.

It opened easily.

"Are you serious?" Max said. His face turned from surprise to anger, and he leaned into the basement. "Nice one, you little bastard. Let's see you get home without me. You and your stupid pranks." He shouldered Tyler on his way out of the kitchen. "I bet you were in on the whole thing, too."

Tyler watched him leave openmouthed. Watched that little ball of light go, leaving him with only darkness.

He stared down the black hole of the basement. "Danny?" he called, but quietly. The footsteps were coming. Slow, but they were coming.

He felt so cold. Icy air blew out from the basement. He couldn't leave Danny down there.

"Danny, I'm coming to get you."

He reached for a banister on the wall, but found nothing but dusty cold stone beneath his hand. The cold air, a wind really, blew his hair back off his forehead. He swallowed, and took a step down into nothingness.

The stair beneath his foot felt spongy and insubstantial.

"Danny?" he called softly.

He stepped down again. His hand brushed against spider webs. The darkness, for all the cold, pressed against his face with clammy hands, and Tyler found breathing difficult. He wanted nothing more than to turn back around. His legs shook as he took another step down.

"Danny, please, if you're there, answer me, please." His voice shook as well.

Behind him, the sparse light from the kitchen seemed far away, a glimmer of hope through an open doorway. It illuminated nothing in the cellar. Tyler moved faster down the stairs. Every time he took a breath, the icy air filled his lungs and made his entire body feel colder. Soon he was barely whispering his pleas to Danny, his lips forming words that made clouds of breath in front of him.

He had to be close to the bottom, he had to be. The steps kept going down and down, like they were descending into a frozen hell. The wall seemed to curve, the stairs curved in a downward spiral. He stopped being so careful. His feet moved down and down and down, unending.

He stumbled when the steps abruptly ended and the ground was flat, and tripped over something on the ground. A solid, soft something that moved when his foot kicked it. He put his hands out in front of him and they collided with a cold stone wall, skinning the heels of his palms.

"Danny? Is that you?"

Tyler crouched and tried to feel the lumpy shape with his hands. It felt like clothes over sack filled with bones. He shook the form. "Danny, wake up."

He couldn't even see what part of his friend he was touching. The rough fabric felt like jeans, so he moved one way, then the other, trying to feel the soft ribbed fabric of Danny's shirt. There it was. He moved up further, and found Danny's face.

Holding one hand over Danny's mouth, Tyler could feel puffs of breath. That was good, he told himself. Danny was just unconscious. He tried to slap Danny's cheek to wake him up, but the impact was muffled by a warm, sticky substance.

Tyler felt it between his fingers. Blood, it's blood, his mind screamed. Still, he held his fingers under his nose and smelled it. It had that coppery scent of blood. Danny was bleeding. He had to get Danny out of there. Why did Max have to run off like that? Tyler was strong, but he wasn't sure he could get Danny up all those stairs.

He had to try. He didn't even want to think about what might have come down from the second floor. Tyler got his hands under Danny's armpits and yanked his limp body up to a sitting position. "Danny, come on, wake up," Tyler muttered.

Creaks walked across the ceiling overhead.

Somehow, in a matter of seconds, Tyler had Danny in a fireman's carry across his shoulders.

Without the aid of his hands, Tyler had to feel around with his foot for the stairs. He shuffled around the landing, unable to find anything except the wall. Panic rose in his throat. He feared he was walking deeper into the basement.

The creaks upstairs stopped immediately over Tyler's head.

A sob escaped his constricted throat. "Please, I'm sorry," he sobbed, unsure of who he was addressing.

His foot hit something. He shuffled forward and stood on one foot to test the object's height. It was a stair! Tears rolled down his face in relief. He started heading upward.

Getting up the stairs was a bit more difficult with Danny's added weight and trying to feel with his sneaker where the stair was.

The creaks upstairs began moving again.

In a panic, Tyler started running up the stairs. Almost immediately he tripped and barely managed not to drop Danny back down the stairs. He caught himself on one knee and painfully got himself upright. The creaks had stopped, but when Tyler started moving again, the creaks also began. Tyler was gasping for air. The cold air stabbed into his lungs.

The door swam into his vision. He didn't know if it had been out of sight, or if his eyes hadn't been looking for it. Light, albeit dim light, coming through the doorway. He thought he could even make out the refrigerator in the moonlight.

The creaks were coming faster, but Tyler could make it. He was a good runner. He could see the escape route now, and he was going to make it.

Two steps from the top of the stairs, the basement door slammed in his face.

Tyler screamed and stumbled, careening into the stone wall. Danny's weight pulled him backwards. Tyler had to press his back and Danny's body up against the wall to keep his balance. He took a few deep breaths, feeling icy tears run down his face.

He had to get out, but what the hell was out there waiting for him?

Tyler stepped up to the door. He balanced Danny on his shoulders and reached out for the doorknob. It was freezing cold and Tyler felt a shiver run up his arm and down his spine. But the knob turned, and the door swung open as easily as before.

The kitchen was empty.

Tyler stared at the empty room for long moments, his heaving breaths the only sound. No creaking. Nothing. He took the final step up into the kitchen, carefully maneuvering Danny's head and legs through the doorway. The door was right there. He could do it. He could get out of this house.

He staggered forward.

***

Once outside of the house and on the road, Tyler dropped to his knees and dumped Danny on the ground. In the weak moonlight he could see that Danny had hit his head when he'd fallen down the stairs. Tyler ripped off a piece of his t-shirt and pressed it against the wound. His shaking fingers found a pulse in Danny's neck.

The night air felt strangely warm after the basement. Tyler's whole body shook out the cold. How was he going to get Danny home? The hike back to the road would take that much longer carrying Danny's weight, and even to get to Tyler's house took half an hour at a run. His only chance was if Danny could wake up. Tyler grabbed Danny by the shoulders and shook the kid so hard Danny's head looked like it was going to roll and snap right off his neck. Tyler laid Danny back down on the ground and put the cloth back on Danny's head. He supposed that shaking someone with a head injury probably wasn't the best thing in the world to do.

Tyler looked up at the house. He wished he could close that front door. Things could escape from the house with it open.

Voices called out in the dark. "Danny!" they called. Faintly, Tyler could see the beams of flashlights swinging in arcs over the trees.

"We're up here!" Tyler yelled, his voice hoarse and barely audible. He stood and waved his arms. "Hello! We're right here!"

Then he sank down to the ground and waited.

Chapter 13

At school on Monday, Tyler anxiously looked for Danny. The last time he'd seen the kid was in Max's car. Mr. Krull had gotten angry at Max for coming home without his brother, and made him go back to the house to get him. They had dropped Tyler off at his house. Danny had still been unconscious.

Tyler wished he had been unconscious when he got home. His parents were awake, waiting for him, all lights in the house blazing. It was two in the morning, much later than Tyler had thought.

"Where have you been?" his mother said. "We've called everyone we could think of. No one knew where you were. How could you lie to us like that?" After a pause, she added, "Have you been drinking?"

He couldn't even deal with it. He slumped up to his room without saying a word. He heard his father say, "He doesn't look good. Maybe something happened."

By the morning—or early afternoon, since Tyler slept until about one, and his parents slept in late too—his mother's anger had worn off. Time for his father to step in. Over a breakfast of eggs and pancakes, while Tyler picked at what he normally would have scarfed down, his father asked, "You didn't go to the dance last night, did you, bud."

Tyler shook his head.

"So what happened?"

He poked at his scrambled eggs. He still felt weird inside, like he wanted to throw up. "I went to this party."

"And was there alcohol involved?"

Tyler nodded.

"That's probably why you don't feel so great, huh. Drinking... it isn't good, kid. Looks like you might have gotten into a fight, too."

Tyler poked more aggressively at his food. The bacon had a sickly sheen to it.

"So you really want to stay away from that kind of thing, okay, sport? Your mom and I agreed that you should be grounded for a while, until you get back on track."

"Fine," Tyler mumbled.

After a few minutes of silence, Tyler got up and dumped his food, and went back to bed.

He was feeling better by Monday. He'd done all his homework, tried to stuff what happened at the house into his subconscious. It seemed less and less real. Probably he'd just been scared, hearing things in the dark. It was easy to remember it that way during the day, when the sun was shining.

At night was a different story. The dark brought back all those memories: the creaking, coming after him; descending the basement stairs and thinking they would never end. Tyler's dreams got him confused: in one, he kept going down and down, until it actually began to get warmer and warmer, and light started flickering on the walls, and then flames coming up. He woke up before he got to the bottom. In another, everywhere he walked, he heard those creaking footsteps following him.

The dream that most freaked him out took place in that little room in the upstairs of the abandoned house, the one with the stained mattress. He was lying on the bed and everything was black, but somehow he knew he was in that little room. Nothing else happened, but it was like he was waiting for something to happen. When he woke up, lying in his bed in his own dark room, it had taken many long minutes before he figured out he was no longer dreaming.

After that, Tyler had broken down and taken a small lamp from Sam's bedroom to leave on at night. Sunday he slept as soundly as normal.

"Hey, Tyler." Mike joined Tyler at his locker. "How was your weekend?"

"It was okay," Tyler said.

"It's too bad you didn't come to the dance. You know Carolyn Kingsley? I totally made out with her half the night."

"Sweet," Tyler said faintly. He peeked around for Danny.

"Hey, there she is," Mike said. "Quick, pretend I said something funny."

"What?"

"Just do it. Laugh or something." When Tyler could only stare blankly at his friend, Mike muttered, "Geez, Tyler, what is your problem today?" Then Mike suddenly smiled, looking over Tyler's shoulder. "Hey, Carolyn."

Tyler almost gagged on a wave of perfume as Carolyn sashayed by. It made him suddenly grateful that Karin didn't have to wear perfume. She smelled nice from her shampoo.

"Hey, Ty, hey Frank."

Mike scrunched up his face in disapproval.

Tyler turned to see Danny, with a giant bandage on his forehead. He also had scrapes all on that side of his face. "Danny! How are you feeling?"

"What happened to you?" Mike said. "Frontal lobotomy?"

Ignoring Mike's comment, Danny hugged Tyler.

"Thank you so much for saving me," he said into Tyler's shirt. Tyler, not expecting the affection, held himself stiff, his face growing hot. When Danny pulled away, his eyes were shining. "Max told me what happened. At first he tried to say that he had rescued me, but then my dad said Max was a liar, and Max spilled the truth. I can't believe you carried me all the way out of there."

"Out of where?" Mike wanted to know.

"Uh..." Tyler wished he could make Danny shut up, before everyone and their brother knew about the abandoned house. But Danny didn't answer Mike either.

"Anyway, Ty—" Danny rubbed his eyes— "I owe you big time. I've never had a friend who would do that for me. I mean, not even my brother! Isn't that crazy? I'm so, so glad to have a best friend like you."

"I'm Tyler's best friend," Mike said, looking to Tyler for confirmation.

Tyler didn't pay any attention to Mike. He took in Danny's wet eyes and quivering chin and the oversized bandage on his forehead. He was relieved that Danny was okay, but he still wasn't sure he wanted Danny as his best friend. Well, he couldn't pop the kid's balloon now. He'd have to let him down easy later on.

Tyler took a deep breath and headed to class, with Mike and Danny following.

***

At lunch, Mike sat on one side of Tyler, and Danny sat on the other. The other kids at the lunch table looked at Danny with confusion, and once they figured out he was Tyler's friend, they started looking at Tyler strangely, too. Karin walked up to where Tyler was sitting with her lunch tray. "Hi, Tyler," she said.

"Hi Karin," Tyler said.

"Um, I guess I'm going to sit down here," she said, moving toward the other end of the table where there were some empty seats.

Tyler stared down at his lunch, wishing Danny would disappear. Or maybe Mike.

"Is that your girlfriend?" Danny asked. "The cheerleader?"

"She's not my girlfriend," Tyler said quietly, hoping Karin wouldn't hear.

"She's smokin'," Danny said. "A stone fox, as my dad would say. A hot mama. A—"

"I get it," Tyler snapped.

"I have a girlfriend," Danny said. He popped open the top of his soda can.

"You do?" He had tried to hide his surprise, but it still came out.

"Of course. Back in Lowell, I was pretty much a pimp." Danny crammed a handful of Doritos in his mouth.

A couple of the guys at Tyler's table snickered. One of them said, "Oh yeah?"

"I'll show you a picture." Danny wiped his hands on his jeans, leaving orange streaks behind, and pulled out his phone. He flipped through a few pictures, kids who looked like Danny's brothers and sisters, and held it out for Tyler to view. "See?"

The girl was Hispanic with full lips and heavy eye makeup. The picture looked like Danny might have copied it off the internet somewhere. "She's pretty," Tyler said lamely.

"She's a hot mama," Danny corrected. "She's also a really good kisser."

Tyler could tell that none of the other kids at the table were buying it. He handed the phone back to Danny.

Instead of putting his phone away, Danny continued to flip through his photos. "This is us at our eighth grade graduation dance," he said. "And these we took at the movies, in one of those little photo booths?"

It did appear as though Danny and the girl were dating. "What's her name?" Tyler asked.

"Jasmine."

"And you're still going out with her even though she still lives in Lowell and you live here?"

"We text and Facetime each other all the time," Danny said.

"Cool," Tyler mumbled. At the other end of the table, Karin laughed at something and tossed her golden hair over her shoulder. She suddenly made eye contact with him and he blushed, looking down at his sandwich.

"So, Dan, you mentioned that Tyler saved your life?" Mike interjected.

"Yeah!" Danny said.

Tyler tried to signal to Danny not to mention the abandoned house, but Danny was too excited to notice.

"My brother was fooling around and I got locked in the basement of this old house. It was totally dark and creepy and I fell down the stairs and I got knocked unconscious. Next thing I knew, Ty was carrying me out of the basement. Everybody else took off, but Tyler went down in the basement to rescue me, without even a flashlight."

Now Tyler really blushed, his face burning. He felt like everyone at the table was staring at him. He didn't even want to see the look of complete adoration Danny was probably beaming at him.

Then Danny said, "It was like those stories you hear about adrenaline rush, right? I mean, who would think a skinny little kid like Ty could pick me up and carry me up a flight of stairs?"

Already Tyler was beginning to regret rescuing Danny from that basement.

Chapter 14

In English class Mrs. Tanner reminded them about their historical house papers, so after school Tyler rode his bike down to his mother's office to see what information she had. He was going to do his paper on his own house—it was the easiest thing to do. His mother had a whole file full of information. It only took him twenty minutes or so to get all the notes he needed for his paper. As he was putting the file away, he noticed a file for Birdsall Drive.

He sneaked a peek at his mother. She was busy with a customer on the phone. He turned so his back was blocking was he was doing, and pulled out the file.

Unlike the other file folders that had typewritten labels and dates, this file's label was handwritten. There was no date. The folder didn't look like it was in bad condition; on the contrary, it appeared to have been barely used.

The pages inside were typewritten, in old-fashioned type:

Birdsall Drive

March 18, 1971

The road needs clearing—abundance of undergrowth, largely obscuring the drive. Land is gently sloping. Soil appears rocky. Dilapidated house about 2.3 miles in; appears abandoned (Note: check for history). The logging site approx. 5 miles has a number of stumps that will need to be removed. Otherwise this site appears ready for construction.

March 22, 1971

The house on Birdsall Drive is still listed as being owned by a Mr. and Mrs. Theodore Birdsall, dated in the 1930s. Their land, according to records, extends into the logging site. Check for their current address, since the house was clearly deserted.

March 30, 1971

Found the death certificates for Mr. or Mrs. Birdsall. Will have to petition Town Hall for permission to purchase land.

May 2, 1971

Land on Birdsall Drive unsuitable for building.

Tyler stared at the last entry. Whoever had done this research had reported earlier that the logging site was perfect for building. Someone had wanted to build a development up there, then completely changed their mind a month later. That date... wasn't 1971 the same year some girl had wandered out of the woods claiming to be Ellen Birdsall? It was too much of a coincidence.

He wondered if Middlebury Realty had gone so far as to buy the land that house was on. Maybe that's why he couldn't find it in the library's index. They might have changed the name of the road legally, but never built anything there. Tyler wondered if they had gone into the house at all.

His mother was still talking on the phone. Tyler carefully slid the Birdsall Drive folder into his backpack.

"Hey, Mom, I'm going to run to the library real quick," he said, and bolted out of the office before she had a chance to say no.

Of all people, Tyler least expected Danny to be hanging out at the library after school. "What are you doing here?" Tyler asked.

"This place has free internet. And my brothers usually hog the computer after school."

"Oh." Tyler supposed it made sense. "Well, I'm going down to the History Room to do some research."

"Bummer," Danny said. "See you later." Tyler left him watching some YouTube video.

Down in the cold jail-like room Tyler flipped the on switch of the microfilm machine and listened to the hum of it warming up as he pulled out a drawer full of microfilm boxes. He selected 1971 and somehow finagled the film through the machine. Pressing the button, months' worth of newspaper articles flew past his eyes. He slowed down and stopped in April.

Scrolling by headlines, Tyler squinted in search of the one about the girl saying she was Ellen Birdsall. It had to be in April. Where was it? He saw an article about building the "new" high school. Another about the town's tri-centennial anniversary celebration. Wait! There it was: Girl Wanders Out of Forest, Claims to be Ellen Birdsall.

"Middlebury, MA – Mrs. James Parker of Pine Hill Road had quite the surprise whilst hanging her laundry yesterday afternoon. 'This girl wandered out of the forest right into my backyard,' Mrs. Parker said. 'I thought she was a ghost.'

"The girl, who appeared to be in her early teens, identified herself as Ellen Birdsall. 'She kept asking about her family, she kept saying, "Where are my mother and father?"' Mrs. Parker told this reporter. She called police, believing the girl to be a runaway or lost.

"While in police custody, 'Ellen' reported that her parents' names were Theodore and Belinda Birdsall, and that they lived in town. The only records police could find for those names were about fifty years old. During this search, police also found that an Ellen Birdsall died of mysterious causes in 1936.

"When confronted with this information, the girl continued to affirm that her name was Ellen Birdsall. Due to the girl's disheveled appearance and her ravings that someone was trying to get her, police sent her to the Willow House, a psychiatric asylum for girls."

On the same page, another smaller headline read, "Search continues for missing woman." Tyler read, "Winifred Lambert, 34, a local land surveyor, disappeared a week ago while mapping out a new building site. Co-workers claim that she had simply vanished. Search teams comprised of police, park rangers, search and rescue dogs, and volunteers, were unable to find any trace of Ms. Lambert. 'We expected this, after all the rain we've been having,' said local park ranger Walter Wozniak. Police now suspect foul play and are now looking for any information as to the whereabouts of Winifred

Lambert. The family is offering a reward of one thousand dollars for information leading to her safe return."

Tyler sat back in the chair. Could this woman have been the reason the site was declared unsuitable for building? He scrolled along further in the newspaper, but did not find any other reference to strange happenings in the woods near Pine Hill Road.

"Whatcha doin'?" came a familiar voice behind him.

Tyler jumped and turned around. "Danny! God, you scared me."

"Yeah, well."

Danny ran his fingers across the spines of old National Geographic magazines. "I, um..." Danny cleared his throat and started over. "I've been having some crazy dreams since the night at that house."

"Yeah?"

"This one I keep having, where I'm in the basement. I know it's the basement even though the whole dream is in the dark. And I mean, black dark. I can't see anything. But I can feel things in the darkness, some kind of presence... and then I feel a hand on my shoulder, behind me, and that's when I wake up."

"Sounds creepy," Tyler said, careful to keep his voice light and steady. He tried to remove the microfilm from the machine nonchalantly, like he was finished and not trying to hide anything.

"And there's another one, I'm lying on this little bed. Just lying there. I can't get up, and it's all dark in this little room, and I know no one will ever come to let me go, and the room keeps getting smaller and smaller and then it's like I'm in a coffin?"

This was too eerily close to the dreams Tyler had been having. He looked down and saw that he had goose bumps on his arms.

"I think that house is really haunted," Danny concluded. "I didn't really believe in ghosts before, but now..."

Tyler kept his eyes on the microfilm box as he carefully put the reel inside. "I saw something there once. A couple days before we all went there."

"Yeah?"

"Or, I thought I saw something. I can't be sure."

"What was it?"

"It looked like a pair of shoes, at the edge of a shadow..." Tyler trailed off, realizing how ridiculous it sounded. "I was really freaked out, that's all. There was probably nothing there. I've been in that house tons of times—"

Tyler stopped.

He had remembered his little fire. Wasn't that what he was doing when those freaky footsteps started up? What if his fire had pissed off something that haunted the place?

"What?" Danny asked.

"I've spent a lot of time in that house and nothing like that ever happened. So it was probably just my imagination."

"Oh." Danny's eyes dropped to the floor.

Tyler knew Danny was looking for someone who didn't think he was a baby for believing the house was haunted. He knew Danny wanted Tyler's acceptance. But Tyler couldn't admit what he'd seen. It was much safer for Danny to forget about the whole thing.

Chapter 15

There was a substitute in math class the next day, which gave Tyler a chance to talk to Karin. He was gearing up to ask her on a date. Preferably on Friday night, so that his sister would have a chance to meet her. Tyler knew Sam would be so proud of him, dating a pretty, nice girl like Karin.

"How was the rest of your weekend?" Tyler asked her. He certainly didn't want to talk about his own weekend, what with the rescuing Danny thing and the getting grounded thing, and especially not the nightmare thing. The best defense was a good offense.

"Pretty boring," she said. "Hey, are you still training for cross country?"

It took Tyler a few moments to figure out what she was talking about. "Oh, yeah. I am."

"Maybe someday after school we could go running together? I really want to get in shape to try out for the spring track season. Where do you usually go?"

He thought about lying to her, but when he glanced up at her trusting eyes, he found himself saying, "This trail, near my house."

"Do you mind if I train with you?" Karin blushed and looked down. "Because if you'd rather train by yourself..."

"No, no, I'd love to train with you. It's always good to have some competition."

"Great! I have cheerleading practice on Mondays, Wednesdays, and Fridays, but how about on Thursday? I can convince my parents we'll be staying on school grounds or something."

"Oh." It took him a moment to realize what she was really saying, and then he felt his face heat up. "They don't want you hanging out with me?"

"It's not you, Tyler," Karin laughed, placing her hand on his arm. He felt like jumping out of his skin every time she touched him. "My parents call anything where I'm alone with a boy 'a date.' And they don't want me dating until I'm thirty."

"But once you're eighteen, can't you—"

Karin laughed again. "You're so funny. I'm totally kidding. They told me I can't date until I'm sixteen. And I can't go to dances until then, either. It's okay, I'll still get to go to the prom and stuff... sometimes I just wish they weren't so strict."

Tyler was relieved that her parents weren't strict because they thought he was a bad influence or not good enough for their daughter or something. "So I guess you wouldn't be able to go to the movies with me this weekend, huh?"

"Well... maybe if we went with Mike and Carolyn and some other kids, like in a big group, they'd be okay with it. As long as it didn't look like a double date. Just a group of friends going to the movies."

"Hmm." Tyler scratched his chin. "Perhaps that can be arranged." He grinned. "Is that a yes? You want to go to the movies with me?"

Karin grinned. "Yes."

For the rest of the day, Tyler felt like he was walking on air.

***

On Thursday afternoon, however, he wasn't feeling so light. In fact, his stomach was tying itself in knots.

He had worn his track pants and running shoes to school in preparation. He figured he and Karin could drop their bags at his house on the way up to the hidden drive. For the past two days he had tried to think of a way to get out of bringing Karin anywhere near the abandoned house. Maybe there was some other trail that he could use. But most of the real hiking trails he could find in town were all on the other side in the state forest. And another part of him was a little excited about showing her the house. They didn't have to go inside. Tyler was sure Karin wouldn't pull a Danny and run into that horrible basement, or the black hole room.

Karin had asked him to meet her outside of the girl's locker room. He imagined her in there, changing out of that baggy sweater she'd worn in class. He wondered what her workout clothes looked like.

He imagined her wearing tight black shorts and a sports bra like the women on the cover of Runner's World.

"Hey, I'm all ready," Karin said. Tyler snapped out of his fantasy to find Karin standing in front of him wearing baggy sweatpants and an old T-shirt that said "Middlebury Middle School" on it, her hair thrown up in a ponytail.

She looked great.

They walked up the road to Tyler's house. Tyler noticed how flushed Karin's face was, but didn't want to ask if it was because she was tired already or if it was because she was excited to be with him. Their shoulders occasionally bumped against each other, and each time she would giggle and he would mumble a bashful apology. Tyler wanted to reach out and hold her hand, but his palms were too sweaty.

"Thc leaves are starting to change," Karin observed.

Tyler looked up at the bright red, orange, and yellow leaves and the clear blue sky.

"It's really pretty," she continued.

Tyler didn't know what to say other than, "Yeah." He felt like the dumbest person alive. Karin would be better off talking to a tree stump.

Instead of talking, Tyler grabbed Karin's hand the next time their fingers brushed against each other. Out of the corner of his eye he saw her smile. His own mouth smiled, too, all the way to his house.

They dropped off their heavy bookbags, then walked along the side of the road to the hidden drive.

"This is the trail?" Karin asked when they got there.

"Yeah. You have to climb through these bushes here."

"Some trail!" Karin laughed. Once they got past the thick of it, she said, "You wanna run?"

In response, Tyler started jogging, slowly at first, then picking up speed as Karin stayed right at his side. Soon they were racing up the hill, dodging loose stones and saplings. This was the part of running that Tyler loved, where he had to focus only on running, and all the other problems in his life faded into a distant background noise. His mind only had to concentrate on where to put his feet.

Only once did he let Karin get ahead of him. For a few long moments he watched her run in front, her honey-blond hair streaming behind her like a flag. Although it wasn't so much her hair he was looking at from behind.

Tyler thought he might be able to get away with running right on by the house. Karin might not even notice the house hidden among the trees and overgrown underbrush.

But Karin slowed down and stopped right in front of it, as if the house had called to her.

"Somebody lives way up here?" she asked when he stopped alongside her.

"No, it's abandoned," he said.

"Really?" She took in the broken windows, the peeling paint. "Have you gone inside?"

"Yeah." Tyler looked up the hill, absently kicking a rock.

He realized that Karin was staring at him raptly. "Really? You've gone inside someone else's house? Weren't you afraid you would get caught trespassing?"

"No." Really, the thought had never crossed his mind. "I mean, you can tell no one's been here in years."

"What's it like in there?"

"It's just a house. There's some old furniture. Nothing big." He shifted his weight from foot to foot. "Hey, um, do you want to—"

"Go inside? Yeah! Do you think it's haunted?"

Tyler was going to say, "Keep on running," but he supposed if he were in Karin's shoes he would be fascinated by the house too. "Um, I don't know..."

"Did you feel any cold spots when you were in there? Because I was watching 'Ghost Hunters' and that's usually a sign that it's haunted," Karin said. She started toward the house, but stopped when Tyler didn't follow her.

The bile was rising in his throat. His body remembered that night, the cold clammy feel of the basement and the terrible crazy feeling that the house was swallowing him whole, that he'd end up wandering around blindly in the basement until he died. He stared at the ground, willing his eyes not to look up at Ellen's bedroom window.

"Tyler? Don't you want to come inside with me?"

"Um... I don't know... I mean, I don't think it's a good idea," he said thickly.

"What do you mean? You said you already went in there."

"I know," he said faintly. He swallowed. "I just... it's kind of creepy."

Karin laughed. "I'm sorry. I mean, it's funny. You're scared!"

He felt heat swim up into his face. "No—no, I'm not, it's just that—"

"You are! You're afraid!"

Tyler couldn't even say anything in defense. He was afraid. He was completely freaked out. Why was he so stupid? Couldn't he have thought of some lie to tell her, some other place to go?

"Oh, come on," Karin said. And she reached out and grabbed his hand and pulled him inside.

Once in the familiar kitchen, Karin didn't let go of his hand, or maybe he didn't let go. Immediately he noticed that the basement door was open. He gripped her hand, feeling the sweat on his palms go cold. Of course the basement door would be open, he told himself. He hadn't stopped to shut it behind him in his race out of the house with Danny unconscious on his shoulders.

Still, a cold breeze seemed to whisper from the basement.

Karin quickly pulled him into the living room. "This is so cool," she murmured. "Why would they leave all this stuff behind?"

Dragging him into the office, Karin said, "What's your theory?"

"Theory?" Tyler maneuvered himself in front of the desk, trying to hide the burned spot.

"Yeah. Why do you think the original owners left this place like this? With all this stuff?"

"Uh... I think their kid died. Like they had a daughter, and then she died all of a sudden, maybe in a horrible accident, and they had to leave the house, because there were too many bad memories." Or maybe because there was a ghost, he almost added, but stopped. Karin already thought he was a wussy baby afraid of a house.

"Really?" Karin slipped her hand out and started leafing through the papers on the desk and floor. "My first guess would have been tax evasion."

"Tax evasion?" The words were too normal to belong to this place.

"Yeah. My father works for the IRS, and nine out of ten times a person owes back taxes or whatever their address has changed and their phone is disconnected. They leave, to escape the government." She looked at him. "Your theory is much more interesting."

"Or maybe it's just more morbid."

"At least your theory leaves the possibility of a ghost. Mine's... boring. It's so boring it's not normal. What normal kid thinks about tax evasion?" Karin sighed in disgust. "Sometimes I feel so weird!"

Tyler laughed. "You? The only thing weird about you is that you're so good at everything."

"My parents would ground me if they ever knew I watched a blasphemous show like 'Ghost Hunters.'" Karin smiled sadly down at the papers in her hands. "They'd kill me if they knew where I was right this second."

All thoughts of a ghost flew out of his head. He moved closer to her, smelled the honey scent of her hair. He peeked over her shoulder at the papers. "My theory might be more exciting, but it looks like yours might be right." Rows of numbers covered the papers.

"These other ones, I think these are from a newspaper," Karin said, pointing to some bits of yellowed paper. Suddenly Karin turned to look at him. "Have you ever kissed anyone?"

It took Tyler a second to react to the change of subject. "Uh... I, uh, no." His face burned. That was smooth, he scolded himself. She'll really want to kiss you now.

Then Karin's lips were on his. Their softness pressed against him with an urgency he didn't understand. He parted his mouth and tasted her sweetness, something in her lip gloss or maybe she simply tasted sweet, breathing in that aroma from her shampoo. His hands moved to her hips, pulled her closer to him, so that more than just their lips met.

Her hands grabbed his t-shirt at first, keeping him locked in the kiss, then they moved to his hair. His body tingled when she pulled her fingers through his hair, and he responded by pulling her closer, onto his lap.

By the time they came up for air, they had both relaxed. Her fingers drifted, traced the edges of his t-shirt. Tyler looked into her gray eyes, and smiled.

Karin leaned forward. "Let's go explore upstairs," she whispered, her breath tickling his ears.

He followed her willingly enough, but when he saw the staircase, he stopped. All the hairs on his arms were standing on end. His spine felt like it was made of ice.

"What's wrong?" Karin asked. He could only look at her. He couldn't say anything. "Are you just trying to freak me out? Tyler?

What's wrong?" She tried to pry her hand out of his grip and couldn't. "Tyler, let go. Your hand is so cold..." She looked into his eyes. He felt a tear slip out of his eye and down his cheek. "You're so pale. You're crying! Is something wrong?"

Her warm hand brushed the tear away, warmed him slightly. "I can't go up there," he croaked. "It's waiting for me. I'm so scared."

"Oh my gosh," Karin said, her eyes shining. "You're so cute!"

His skin hardened into ice again.

"You put on such a macho act, and you're all afraid of a little old abandoned house."

His stomach felt like a roiling mess inside, but it was like he was trapped inside of a hard shell. He was holding Karin's hand but felt miles away from her.

"I'm just kidding. Let's go upstairs."

The voice sounded like his own, but he hadn't felt his mouth moving. He couldn't feel his mouth at all. It was completely numb. He tried to touch his lips, to make sure they were still there, but his hand wouldn't move.

And then he was floating forward on someone else's legs. He felt himself pulled along behind Karin like some kind of balloon. Not upstairs, please, not upstairs, not into that room.

Slowly, as he drifted up the stairs, the ice melted. Golden sunlight streamed in through the holes in the roof and created a halo out of Karin's blond hair. Looking at her, he felt completely safe. He didn't know how he could have imagined something like a pair of black shoes. There was nothing here.

"Which room should we go in?" Karin asked coyly, looking over her shoulder at him.

He smiled back at her. "You choose."

She pulled him up to the second floor and peeked into the first door on the left. "This one looks nice," she said.

Tyler suddenly noticed that all the doors were open. The room across from Ellen's, and the black hole room. It made sense, of course: the last time he'd been here, he hadn't even gone upstairs, and he was sure that Max and Danny and their friends hadn't done something so considerate as close the doors in an abandoned house. Tyler had heard them from the living room, banging around. He wondered how many of them had gone into that little room.

Neither door looked quite so ominous in the sunlight, so Tyler tried to shrug it off. To smile and be with Karin as she pulled him into Ellen's room.

As soon as he passed over the threshold, Tyler's body immediately warmed. His limbs felt so heavy, his hand slipped out of Karin's. He collapsed onto the stained, sagging mattress, breathing in air that warmed his lungs.

"You're tired already? No wonder you didn't make the track team. Good thing I'm here to whip you into shape," Karin said. She sat down at the vanity and looked at herself in the cracked mirror. "It's funny, I look so old-fashioned in this mirror."

Tyler sat up. Hadn't the mirror been broken before? Now the mirror was intact, cracked, but someone had placed all the pieces back together like a sharp puzzle. Had he done that? Now that he thought about it, he could barely remember any of the time he had spent up in this room. The broken beer bottle had been cleaned up at some point too.

Karin pulled open a drawer. "Look, they even left a library book in here," she said, pulling out a copy of Rebecca.

"Oh, that's mine," Tyler said quickly. He had completely forgotten about it.

"Really?" Karin looked at him doubtfully. "You like reading stuff like this?"

Tyler shrugged. "I guess."

Karin smiled and tossed the book onto the bed beside him. "That's what I like about you, Tyler. You've got this secret sensitive side."

Sensitive? Tyler read the back of the book in his hands. He barely remembered reading it. Turned out it was a ghost story. He wondered if that was why he had picked it. He stuck the paperback into the front pocket of his hooded sweatshirt, hoping it wasn't overdue.

"I was wondering why you liked me," Tyler said. "I mean, you're way smarter than me."

Karin swung around to face him, smiling. "You are so funny! We're in all the same classes. You're just as smart as I am." A dimple marked her left cheek. He'd never noticed.

"I guess," he said doubtfully.

"What I really like about you," Karin continued, "is that you're so mysterious."

"Huh?"

He watched as Karin pulled out her ponytail, letting that hair fall over her shoulders and down her back. She turned back to the mirror, picked up the silver-handled hairbrush out of the drawer—had he put that there, or was that another casualty of bringing all those stupid kids here?—and started brushing her hair with long strokes.

"I hardly know anything about you," Karin said, watching him in the mirror. "I know I talk a lot, but even when I ask you about yourself, you change the subject. I can't even begin to imagine what you might be hiding."

He looked away. A history of pyromania, a stint in juvie, punching out new kid on the first day of school... he'd been careful not to breathe a word of any of it, and he wasn't about to start now. He resigned himself to having an air of mystery.

"But I know at least one of your secrets," Karin said, throwing him into a silent, hidden panic.

"You do?"

She laughed. "This house, silly!"

He blushed and tried to smile back.

"Do you think this room belonged to that girl you were talking about? The daughter who died?"

"Maybe," Tyler said.

If he only looked at her back, and made his vision blur a little bit, he could almost see Ellen sitting there, humming to herself, imagining herself to be a movie star.

"What was she like?" Karin asked dreamily.

Tyler looked up at the cracked and water-stained paint on the ceiling, and began to tell the story of Ellen Birdsall.

Chapter 16

"She was fragile, like a baby bird, like my grandmother's china, delicate. But beautiful. Her eyes were the color of the sky. She was too beautiful to be living in the city. And the doctors said her disease would get better with fresh air. Her parents gave up their work in the factories, and her father took a job with a logging company."

He closed his eyes, seeing the story unfold before him.

"Ellen and her parents lived in a tiny apartment over a woodworking shop. The sawdust was always in their lungs, and Ellen's disease became worse. She coughed all the time. Her father worried even more than her mother, because it was the Great Depression and the logging company had gone bankrupt. Her father pretended every morning that he was still going off to work, and Ellen and her mother believed him because every night he came home covered in sawdust and sweat.

"Just before the winter came that year, the father revealed his secret: he had built a house for them up in the woods, along the logging road, and they could live there and not have to pay rent. The best part about the house was that the land had a magical power about it. He said that his back pain had completely disappeared, and he knew that Ellen would get better too. The family agreed to move out there."

There came a creak, accompanied by the mattress dipping under Karin's weight. He felt her curl her long body against his, but with his eyes closed, it was all too easy to imagine that it was Ellen, and she was whispering the words to the story in his ear.

"It was a hard winter, and there wasn't enough money for food. Ellen's health got worse. Near the end, Ellen's father invited Ellen's friend Lily over. The mother thought he might have been trying to raise his daughter's spirits enough for her to get well again, but the father had other plans. After Ellen and his wife had gone to bed for the evening, he snuck into the guest bedroom that he had prepared for this time and strapped Lily to the bed, gagging her so she couldn't make any noise. The next morning he told Ellen and her mother that Lily had gotten homesick in the middle of the night and he had taken her home. They were isolated enough at the house that they never heard about the search parties that went looking for Lily. A few days later, Ellen died, and the police decided that her parents were too distraught to have had anything to do with Lily's disappearance.

"Ellen's mother's grief was real. She watched as her daughter's coffin was buried, and blamed her husband. In reality, her husband had buried Ellen's body in the basement, where the magical force he'd felt was strongest. Every night, he crept into the guest room and prayed over Lily that Ellen's soul would come back to them in Lily's body.

"Maybe Lily finally went crazy from being trapped in that little room with very little food to eat, or maybe Ellen's soul did come back. Maybe Ellen's father had gone crazy. Whatever the case, Lily started looking like Ellen, her long brown curls growing straighter and blonder. Her green eyes turned blue. Ellen's father took out the gag, and she called him Daddy. He was so happy that he immediately untied her hands.

"But something had gone wrong. If it was Ellen, her soul had cracked from coming back through from the other side. She strangled her father, and when her mother heard the commotion and came running, she killed her mother too. She hadn't thought far enough ahead, though. Her father had left handcuffs locking her feet to the bed frame. She tried everything to get her feet out of there. She searched her father's body for keys, but they had fallen beyond her reach. She died there in that room, with the bodies of the parents she had murdered."

Tyler opened his eyes. Where had that come from? He felt Karin gripping his shirt, her eyes wide. "Sorry," he said. "I guess I got a little carried away."

"Did you make that up just now?" Karin asked.

"Yeah, I guess so." In his mind, he heard a sweet girl's voice whispering those words, She died there in that room... He knew how crazy it would sound if he told that to Karin, though.

"Wow. You should be a writer. I could never make something like that up. It's like a Stephen King story or something!"

Tyler blushed at the compliment. He was a little horrified at his story, but somehow it had impressed Karin. He shrugged. "I'm not a good writer, though. English is my hardest class."

"No way. You're so smart," Karin said, snuggling up to his chest. She inhaled—he worried for a moment that he had forgotten to put on deodorant—and added, "Doesn't the sun make you want to curl up and take a nap?"

The afternoon sun was slanting in through the warped windows, casting a warm square on the bed where they lay. "Yeah," he said, closing his eyes again. He wrapped his arms around her.

The lack of truth in his story comforted him. That feeling of Ellen whispering in his ears, that was a trick of his mind. He remembered reading about Ellen's parents in that file he took from the real estate office.

Stealing—another thing to be "mysterious" about with Karin.

There were death certificates for Ellen's parents. So someone must have found them. And Tyler had seen their tombstones with his own eyes. He couldn't remember the dates on them right now, but he was pretty sure it was years after Ellen had died.

For long moments the only sounds were birds twittering outside, small creaks as the breeze fluttered through the house, a dripping into the buckets downstairs. Tyler felt time start to flow away, ticking along with Karin's slow and steady breathing. The sun on his face felt nice—he could almost forget the approaching chill of autumn, and the fear of cold that seemed to suddenly loom over him.

He must have dozed off, because a creak that was more of a squeal jolted him. His entire body tensed, and his eyes snapped open.

Why had that one little sound jerked him awake, when he'd been listening to the sounds of the house settling? Goosebumps had pricked up all along his arms, too. He opened his eyes into dimness. Probably because the sun had gone down behind the trees, or behind a cloud. The redness of the light coming through the warped panes made him think it must be late.

"Karin?" he whispered, shifting his arm out from underneath her. She rolled off, still sleeping, curled up in a ball facing away from him.

The creak came again, only it wasn't the usual short creak; it lasted a minute, maybe more, became a low howl or groan that involved the entire house. All around him Tyler felt the house moaning.

"Karin? Karin, wake up. Please wake up." He shook her so hard that her body flopped loosely around on the bed, but her eyes remained closed. "Oh God Karin, please wake up."

A door slammed. The sound echoed like a rifle shot.

He jumped. He tried to get a hold of himself. It was probably the wind, he thought. The wind must have come in through the hole in the roof, or through the broken window panes, and blown the door shut. Even before he looked out the window and saw the still calm of the world outside that completely went against the intense creaking of the house, he remembered opening those doors, and how they seemed to

—stick—

Then the footsteps began.

It terrified him, even more than before. Maybe because he was trapped here in this room if whatever belonged to those footsteps came in here. He didn't have much time to escape, and even if he did make it out of the bedroom, he would find himself face to face with whatever it was.

He jabbed Karin with his elbow. "Wake up," he said, his voice rising far above a whisper. He grabbed her by both shoulders and shook her violently, her head snapping back and forth. "Wake up!" he screamed in her face.

Her eyes remained closed, her face relaxed and peaceful. And suddenly, Tyler was afraid that she would wake up, that her eyes would be some other color than gray. That something else would be inside of her.

He let her body fall back down onto the mattress, and backed up as far as he could. His back against the wall. Maybe he could still run and make it. Maybe he could get out, even if he left Karin here. It would be better to bring someone back to help her, he thought, knowing it would take far too long, Karin would never survive if he left her here.

The room grew darker, even though the sun was still dim outside. Tyler blinked and rubbed his eyes, thinking he was in the process of blacking out. No, it wasn't his eyes. The room was getting darker. And he thought he could see the darkness rising, creeping into Ellen's room from the hallway, foreboding of that thing out there.

Could he make it? Every nerve in his body itched to run, to dash out there, don't look down the hallway to see it, whatever it was, Ellen or Lily or some crazy cracked soul seeking vengeance, just keep his head down and run. He wanted it so badly that he saw it happening, saw himself running down the stairs, heard the sound it would make, his sneakers exciting loud squeals from the old wood, the softer sound on the living room floor because of the rot in the boards.

Yet his body refused to move.

His muscles had tensed into painful knots, his legs curled up to his chest, his arms clutching them tight with his hands in fists, his knuckles digging into his legs and his fingernails cutting into his palms. He heard a high squeaking sound and didn't even realize that it was his teeth grinding together between his clenched jaws.

Something about the growing darkness seemed to turn the corner, it seemed to be right there, but it was too dark to see anything. His body felt the presence, the hairs on his neck stood on end, his muscles clenched even more tightly, as though it could protect Tyler. His half-blind eyes darted to Karin's sleeping form, looking so open and exposed. He couldn't help her, he couldn't save her. Then, in the doorway—

"Tyler? Wake up."

He was screaming. He hadn't even seen it but he was screaming. He brought his hands up to his face, tried to cover his eyes and his ears at the same time, screaming and screaming.

"Tyler! Tyler, wake up!"

It was touching him. Its hands were on him, its fingers digging into his skin. What was it going to do to him?

"Tyler? Wake up! You're having a nightmare!"

Tyler stopped screaming and cracked his eyes open.

The room was back to being bright, although the long shadows of the trees indicated that sun set was close at hand. Karin was leaning over him, her hair golden in the light, her gray eyes concerned. "Are you okay?" she asked.

He forced his body to relax. He forced himself to breathe. He forced himself to answer her. "Yeah, I'm okay."

"You were screaming." Karin sat back, her face doubtful.

"I was?"

"It really frightened me."

Tyler rubbed at his hot cheeks. "Sorry."

Karin stood and wandered back to the vanity. Her hair was a mess, all tangled in a sexy kind of way. Tyler took the opportunity with her back turned to try to check his own hair, make sure it wasn't sticking up in back. And try to shake off that awful dream.

When he turned his attention back to Karin, she was staring at herself in the mirror, her hands exploring her face, touching her hair. "I look different than I remember," he heard her say to herself.

What a weird thing to say, he thought. Out loud he asked, "How do you remember yourself looking?"

"I don't know... it's been so long." Karin looked so sad all of a sudden that Tyler was compelled to get off the bed and hug her. He breathed in the lavender scent of her shampoo.

Instead of turning to kiss him, like he'd hoped, Karin started to cry.

"What's the matter?" he asked.

"I'm so confused," she sobbed.

"About what?"

"I don't know..."

She wasn't making any sense. It seemed like the perfect opportunity to get her out of the house. "Let's go," he said. She submitted to him docilely, following him downstairs and outside like a timid lamb. Once outside, she blinked in the sun, her eyelashes heavy with tears.

"I'd forgotten what the sun looked like," she said.

"Yeah, the house can have that effect on you," Tyler muttered. He was still waking up at night convinced he was in the pitch black of the basement until his eyes adjusted. "Do you still want to run?"

"Run? Why?" Karin looked at him with wide eyes.

"Never mind," he said. "Let's get you home."

As Tyler led her back down the hill, she turned her head to look over her shoulder at the house.

Chapter 17

On the walk to Tyler's house, Karin gazed up at the trees and stated, "It's autumn already."

"Yeah," Tyler said. It was all he could think of to say. Didn't she remember talking about how pretty the leaves were earlier?

At Tyler's house, she stopped. "Where are we?" she asked.

Now Tyler was starting to get worried. "This is my house."

"Oh." She walked inside willingly; he wondered if maybe she had just forgotten what his house looked like. Then she stood in the kitchen looking around like they hadn't been here just an hour or so ago. When Tyler picked up her pink backpack and held it out to her, she stared blankly at it. "Is that mine?" she asked.

"It's not mine," Tyler joked.

Karin didn't laugh. She held it in her hand by one strap, staring at it, until Tyler helped her put it over her shoulders.

Earlier Tyler had wondered if Karin would want him to walk her back to school for her parents to pick her up, considering how they didn't seem to want her hanging around alone with boys. He didn't know how nervous she was about her parents seeing her walking alone with him. But the way Karin was standing there, gazing around at his kitchen, he decided it would be a good idea to walk her back to school and wait with her. She followed him without question, and he couldn't think of anything to say to her. Conversation with Karin had never been hard before—at least, not for her. She was always chattering away while he struggled to think of interesting things to say.

Tyler walked her around to the front of the school to wait for her parents. She gazed around at the building with wide eyes.

"Um, do you want me to wait here with you?"

"What are we waiting for?" she asked.

"Your parents? They're coming to pick you up."

"They are? Oh, that's wonderful. I feel as though it's been such a long time since I last saw their faces."

Tyler gave her a weird look, then restated his question. "Do you want me to stay with you?"

"I don't mind," she said, and smiled at him.

There was something so ethereal and beautiful about her smile, he couldn't quite figure out what it was. All he knew was that she was smiling at him, and it made his own face light up. They waited for quite some time. Some kids that Tyler knew came out the front door. "Hey, Tyler," they said as they passed and walked toward the McDonald's across the street. They gave him a thumbs up. It seemed like everyone knew about him and Karin.

"Tyler," Karin murmured, touching a finger to her lips. "It fits you perfectly."

"It does?"

She seemed startled that he had heard her. "Y-yes." She blushed. "It's a beautiful name. So unusual." She smiled at him.

Unusual? he thought. Maybe for Middlebury. In Lowell there had been at least three other kids named Tyler at his school.

"So, um, you don't think your parents will be upset that you're hanging around with a boy all alone?" Tyler asked. He was worried. The last thing he wanted was for Mr. and Mrs. Grady to order Karin never to see him again. He had already gotten Mike and everyone together to go to the movies tomorrow night.

"Well, they might be a little upset," Karin said. "But you seem polite and kind, so I doubt they will mind. I mean, aren't we beyond the old days when girls needed chaperones all the time?"

Time to give her another weird look. "I guess we are," he said slowly.

"Of course, Mother and Father are quite old-fashioned. And somewhat strict. Still, I think they are past the point of believing every girl needs a chaperone."

"Okay," Tyler had said, trying to stop her from talking. She sounded so weird.

Finally a minivan pulled up in front of Tyler and Karin. Tyler looked at Karin, who stared at the vehicle and didn't move. "So, I'll see you tomorrow night?" he asked.

"That's so odd." Karin's voice was dreamy.

Tyler glanced at the woman behind the minivan's steering wheel. The woman was looking at Karin with her eyebrows raised, gesturing for Karin to get in.

"I think she wants you to get in," Tyler said, nudging Karin with his elbow.

"Why?"

"Um, to take you home? Isn't that your mom?"

Karin refocused on the woman inside the van. "No." She shook her head. "That's not my mother."

Tyler glanced uncertainly at the woman in the van, who was now waving her arm as if trying to get Karin's attention. "It sure looks like she knows you."

"No. That is certainly not my mother," Karin said.

The van's window rolled down. "Karin Elizabeth Grady, what are you waiting for? It's time to go. I have to pick your sister up from ballet in less than five minutes."

Karin turned and looked behind her.

"Karin! Get in the car. Now."

Tyler cleared his throat to get Karin's attention. "Um, I think you should go with her."

"But she's not my mother," Karin said. She pleaded with her eyes.

A high pitched beeping went off as the woman got out of the van and stalked over to where they stood. "You don't want to get in the car? Fine. We'll do this here," Tyler heard her mutter. He kept his eyes on the ground.

Mrs. Grady stuck her finger right in Karen's face. "What are you doing here with this boy? I thought you had an extra cheerleading practice."

Karin cowered from her mother and looked to Tyler for help. "I—I don't know—"

The slap was so loud, even Tyler flinched. "You know I don't approve of you being alone with a boy without an adult present," Mrs. Grady said. "How could you lie to me?"

"I'm sorry!"

"Get in the car."

"I'm sorry, please!"

Karin was crying, he could hear it in her voice. He couldn't deal with this. He started backing away.

"Get in the car!" As Karin scurried around to get in the passenger seat, Mrs. Grady whirled on him. "And don't think you're getting away scot-free! Get over here!"

Reluctantly, he walked over to Mrs. Grady. He hoped Karin couldn't see his fear that she would hit him, too.

"You are not to speak to my daughter again," Mrs. Grady said. "You are clearly not the sort of boy my daughter should be around."

Tyler's face burned. Out of the corner of his eye he saw the kids milling around the school entrance waiting for their rides watching the whole incident.

"Yes, ma'am," he said.

Mrs. Grady didn't say another word. She got in the van, slammed the door shut, and drove away. Tyler caught a glimpse of Karin as the minivan drove away, but she had her face buried in her hands.

"Whoa, that was intense," said one of kids by the entrance.

Tyler glared at him, and headed home.

***

A bad mood hung over him all evening. He couldn't believe Karin's mother had slapped her. His hands curled into fists every time he thought of that woman lashing out at her own daughter. His mood was so foul that when his mother couldn't stop babbling about their plans for Sam's weekend home, he asked to be excused from the table.

On his way up the stairs, he slammed his fist in the wall, not hard to enough to go through the plaster, but enough to scrape up his knuckles. Normal parents might come and ask what was wrong, or yell at him not to destroy their house. His parents stopped talking, but did nothing. He slammed the door to his room, but he could still hear them pick up their conversation right where it left off.

He should have stood up to Mrs. Grady. He should have punched her right in her face, show her how it feels to get hit. Yes, that's what he should have done. But what had he done? Nothing. Stood there and agreed never to even talk to Karin again.

Rage boiled inside of him. It had been a long time since he felt this way. What had that stupid therapist told him to do when he felt his anger get out of control? Punch a pillow, take deep breaths? He forced air in and out of his lungs through his teeth, but it only charged him, made him angrier. He kicked his bed post. He punched his mattress. His fist sprung back at him. He punched his bureau and succeeded in making his knuckles bleed.

Running usually calmed him, but he knew his legs couldn't take much more running today, after both gym class and his run with Karin. Before that time in the basement, being in the house had made him feel calm. He didn't think it would work anymore.

The only other thing that calmed him was fire.

Tyler paced in his room, trying to work off his anger. It wasn't working. He was going to explode. He reached into his nightstand, into a cigar box full of odds and ends, and took out the lighter. The orange tube rolled in his fingers for a few moments, then Tyler decisively stuck it in his pocket and tore open the door to his room.

"I'm going for a run," he told his parents as he went out the back door, not giving them any time to say, Maybe that's not a good idea, it's late.

He didn't care.

When he was deep enough into the woods, he put together a small campfire, even building a little fireplace out of rocks. He crouched and lit a fistful of leaves and pine needles. The fire nibbled at the fall foliage. He piled on small twigs, then larger sticks and finally some good-sized branches. He squatted beside the fire, the flames consuming his vision.

The blaze cleared out his mind. There, underneath the cloud of emotions, lay the truth about Karin.

How could he have been so stupid to think that she really liked him? A guy like him had nothing to offer a girl like that. He wasn't smart enough, or attractive enough. He couldn't beat her in a foot race.

The only reason someone as perfect as Karin Grady would go after someone like Tyler was to rebel against her parents.

It made sense. She'd probably known the entire time that he'd punched a kid on the first day of school. Maybe she'd even heard rumors that he was a pyro, from whoever told Danny. She always complained about how her parents never let her do anything. It must have been so exciting for her, to disobey their rules and sneak off into an abandoned house with someone they definitely would not approve of. Someone like Tyler.

There he was, feeling sorry that Karin's mother slapped her, when Karin had only been using him.

There he was, thinking that Karin was as beautiful as Ellen, who was so good and kind that her parents died trying to keep her alive. Ellen, who had reached beyond the grave to make him feel welcome, and all he'd done was burn a hole in her father's desk and invite a bunch of stupid kids there to wreck the place.

By the time the fire burned itself out, Tyler's legs were sore from squatting there. His anger had burned out, replaced by a desolate heaviness. He walked home in the darkness, too tired to think.

Chapter 18

Karin wasn't in school on Friday. Tyler chewed on his fingernails all day, wondering where she was. What if that woman really hadn't been Karin's mother? What if Karin had been kidnapped?

"Hey, Frank, wait up!" Tyler ran to catch up with Mike, who had actually turned around when Tyler had called him Frank. "Hey, look, I don't know if tonight's still on, I mean, I have to call Karin and see. Her mom seemed kind of pissed yesterday."

"Oh man, that's bad news," Danny said, coming up behind them.

"Yeah, so anyway," Tyler said, "my sister's visiting from college, so I'll probably just hang out with her tonight if Karin can't go."

"Understandable," said Mike. "I heard some kids talking about how they saw Karin and her mom fighting in the parking lot yesterday. She's tough. But hey, give me a call and let me know how things go, okay?" Patting Tyler on the shoulder, Mike headed out to his bus.

"So you're not doing anything tonight? You wanna go back up to that house?" Danny asked.

Tyler stared at Danny, the huge bandage still on his forehead. "Are you serious?"

Danny shuffled his feet. "I kind of think I might have possibly dropped my brother's cell phone in the basement."

"What?"

"See, he hasn't been able to find his phone, and he says he gave it to me Friday so I could text message Jasmine, because my phone was dead, which I remember, but I can't remember if I gave it back to him or not, and I'm thinking if I didn't give it back to him before we went out to that house, then it could have fallen out of my pocket when I fell down the stairs."

Tyler took a deep breath. "Danny, I really don't want to go back down there."

"I know."

"Maybe you don't remember how bad it was."

"I do, I mean, but if we have a flashlight or something and we can see, it'll be okay. Things look scarier in the dark."

"I don't know about tonight. I'm still grounded, remember?"

"Come on, dude, Max is so pissed at me. He won't even let me use his Playstation."

Tyler didn't see how Danny's lack of Playstation time was worse than going back into that awful basement. "If I see a chance to get away this weekend, I'll call you. But my sister is visiting, so I'm pretty much stuck with my family. Maybe after school on Tuesday."

"I guess I could get Max to go out there with me," Danny said, heading for his bike. "I'm just scared that he'll leave me down there again, and I know you wouldn't do that to me."

Danny sounded so pathetic that Tyler felt bad. "I'll call you if I get a chance to sneak away," Tyler said.

"Great!" Danny unlocked his bike and hopped on. "See you later!"

How did that kid always get his way?

***

He was surprised to see Sam's little green Ford Focus in the driveway when he got home. He ran inside to find her watching soap operas on TV. Actually, all he could see of her was her long sandy brown hair poking out from underneath an afghan. Make that two or three afghans. And make that napping, rather than watching TV.

Tyler snuck up on her and then yelled, "Sam!" right in her ear.

She woke up with a shriek, then hit him with the pillow from under her head. "Geez, I almost thought I missed you. Guess I was wrong."

Tyler gave her a hug.

"Ack, stop it. You know I hate hugging," Sam whined, sitting up and trying to smooth her hair down. A big chunk still stuck out in the back. "I just needed a nap."

"I didn't think you'd be home so early," Tyler said. "And why are you watching this crap?"

"You don't know what it's like, being at college. I have so much free time. Like, classes are only for maybe three hours a day, if I don't skip.

And my homework doesn't take that long. So I've been watching a lot of TV, and taking naps every afternoon... it's great. Of course, I probably wouldn't take naps so often if I didn't stay up until one or two in the morning, but that's when everyone hangs out."

"Sounds cool," Tyler said. "Mom and Dad always yell at me if I stay up too late, even on the weekends. Like if it's two seconds past ten."

"Are you going to be around tonight?"

This reminded Tyler about the situation with Karin. "Um, I'm not sure. I kind of made a date with this girl, but I think her parents aren't going to let her go. I have to call her." Tyler grabbed the cordless phone from its docking station and headed up to his room.

Behind him, Sam said in a high voice, "Oooh, Tyler's got a girlfriend." Then she lay back down.

Tyler had to look up the Gradys' phone number. He hoped Karin was allowed to talk to boys on the phone.

"Hello, Grady residence."

Oh God, it was Mrs. Grady herself.

"Hi, um, this is Tyler McCracken, I'm Karin's friend from school?"

"Yes?" Mrs. Grady said tightly.

"Well, she, uh, wasn't in school today, and she was going to go to the movies with a bunch of us tonight, and I didn't know if she was sick or if she was still coming?"

"No, Tyler, she is quite ill and she will not be leaving the house."

"Oh." He sensed that Mrs. Grady was about to hang up the phone, so he said quickly, "Is she okay? She was acting kind of weird yesterday, I mean, I was wondering what she was sick with?"

"She'll be fine," Mrs. Grady said curtly and hung up.

Tyler pulled the dial tone away from his ear and stared at the phone in his hand. Something was really wrong. Quickly Tyler called Mike and let him know about the change in plans.

"Yeah, Mrs. Grady's really strict," Mike said. "When Karin was going through chemo, she was even worse."

"Chemo?"

"Yeah, didn't you know? I guess you wouldn't. You didn't move here until like fifth grade, right? Yeah, Karin had leukemia in second grade. She missed a ton of school, but on the days when she did come to school, her mother always came in and asked the teacher for the work Karin had missed and made sure Karin's grades were good. Most parents with a kid that sick probably would have had their kids held back a grade or whatever. Not Mrs. Grady. I mean, half the year, Karin didn't even have any hair."

Tyler swallowed. "Wow..."

After Mike hung up, all Tyler could think about was that story he had told Karin about Ellen, how she had been sick and died. He wished he had never opened his mouth. Karin had been so nice and didn't even say anything.

Through his embarrassment, he still felt his anger at Mrs. Grady growing. Ellen's mother never would have treated Ellen that way. Didn't Mrs. Grady know that Karin could have a relapse? On second thought, maybe that was why Karin was acting so weird.

"Hey, I have to clean my room before my mom will let me go out," Mike said, interrupting Tyler's thoughts. "I'll talk to you later, okay?"

"Yeah," said Tyler glumly.

He moped downstairs and sat on Sam's legs under the afghan. "No date?" Sam asked.

He shook his head.

"That's great!" Sam said, sitting up again.

"Huh?"

"Yeah! A bunch of my friends are coming over tonight and we're gonna watch old horror movies."

Sam seemed so excited that Tyler didn't want to mention that their mother had her own plans for what Sam was doing tonight.

***

It turned out that Tyler's mother was so excited about Sam being home that she didn't really care about Sam inviting people over, as long as she was spending the night at home rather than at a friend's house. "Now that Sam's home, we eat like kings," Tyler's father said to him over the steak dinner.

Sam's friends showed up after dinner. Laura and Summer were two girls Tyler had known for a long time. They didn't seem to mind Tyler hanging out in the den with them. Sam put on an old horror movie called, "The Changeling," but none of them seemed interested in watching it. They were too busy comparing notes about college life.

"Everyone starts their weekend on Thursday night," Laura said. "Hardly anyone is in my eight o'clock class on Friday morning."

"I got so drunk last weekend I blacked out," Summer said.

For some reason these confessions bothered Tyler. He'd always thought of Sam and her friends as being so good and perfect. He thought of his own drunken weekend and he couldn't imagine Sam fitting in with that crowd. He scrunched himself down in his bean bag chair and tried to focus on the movie.

The plot followed a man whose family died in a car accident, who goes to live in a big old house by himself to get away from the tragedy. But the house is haunted. The man has this rubber ball that had belonged to his son, and he hides it in a desk drawer because the memory becomes too painful. Then, out of nowhere, the ball comes bouncing down the stairs.

"Boo!" Sam yelled, grabbing Tyler's shoulders.

"Ahhh!" he screamed. The bag of popcorn he'd been gripping in his hands went flying.

Sam and her friends laughed. "That was great. You were so into that movie, your eyes were as big as saucers."

"Very funny," Tyler muttered, getting down on the floor to pick popcorn kernels up off the rug.

By the time he had picked up all the pieces and returned to the den, the lights were off and it looked like the girls had finally gotten into the movie.

Now the man had called a psychic to come and figure out why the house was haunted. The psychic started scribbling on a piece of paper while she asked questions of the spirit. When the spirit answered, her hand jerked and wrote out his answer. There was also a special machine that amplified noises so they could hear and record the spirit too. But Tyler was more interested in the automatic writing.

He knew he had heard of it somehow, allowing the spirit to take control of your hand so it can communicate. He wondered if anyone could learn how to do it. And if he could learn how to do it, maybe he could somehow use it...

Chapter 19

Tyler hadn't been sure that Sam remembered his birthday until she woke him on Saturday morning loudly singing (or screeching) "Happy Birthday."

He cracked his eyes open. Sam was standing there with a bagel with a candle stuck into one side. It was the most pitiful thing he'd ever seen.

"What time is it?" he asked, rubbing his eyes.

"Late enough. Mom woke me up vacuuming at the crack of dawn. She told me to get you out of bed before you sleep your whole life away."

Tyler's alarm clock said it was a quarter to nine.

He hadn't gone to bed until close to two in the morning. After "The Changeling," Sam had put in another horror movie, this one a bit more recent. Then the movie's sequel. She'd still looked wide awake when he dragged himself off to bed without even brushing his teeth.

"So how am I supposed to blow out the candle if it's not lit?" Tyler asked, propping himself up on one elbow.

"I was going to light it," Sam said. "But I couldn't find matches or a lighter anywhere." Her cheeks blushed; they both knew the reason for that.

In a low voice, Tyler said, "I have a lighter."

"You do?" Sam sounded a bit nervous.

Tyler reached into the drawer in his nightstand and pulled it out. He stared at it, this little orange tube that could make fire. The fire on the desk in that house burned its way into his memory.

He carefully handed the lighter to Sam.

She glanced at the doorway to Tyler's room. They could both hear their mother downstairs, vacuuming. Sam turned back to the bagel and flicked the flint with her thumb. Tyler swallowed, watching the flame dance from the lighter over to the candle. When Sam held out the plate for him to blow it out, Tyler hesitated a moment, then puffed a breath that extinguished the flame.

"What'd you wish for?"

"I can't tell you, or it won't come true."

"Fine," Sam pouted. "Here, eat your freaking bagel." She dumped it, candle and all onto Tyler's bed.

"Hey!"

"Whatever," she said leaving the room with the plate. "Mom says you have to change your sheets and vacuum even though it's your birthday. No special treatment."

Tyler stared at the crumbs on his bed. No kidding he wasn't getting special treatment. Never in his life. He grabbed fistfuls of sheets in his hands and yanked them off his bed.

It wasn't until much later that he realized Sam had never given back his lighter.

***

Tyler's birthday was a small affair. Just his parents and Sam. He waited to see how his mother would light the candles on his cake without matches, but somehow she managed to do it out of his sight, and he didn't see how.

His lips tightened and his fists clenched against his legs under the table. Suddenly, now that Sam was home, he remembered how it had been for so long after "the incident." The way his mother had insisted upon an electric stove at their house in Middlebury, how all the candles had mysteriously disappeared, along with the means to light them.

He smiled tightly while everyone sang "Happy Birthday," then quickly blew out the candles.

There was the usual array of presents: clothes and a new video game from his parents, a funny T-shirt from Sam. Then his father said, "I have a surprise."

"What?" he asked.

His mother pursed her lips, then said, "Yes, dear. What is this surprise?"

Whoa, he thought. Even his mother didn't know about this.

"Follow me." His father had a huge grin on his face. Tyler's heart was racing now. He followed his father out into the garage.

Whipping off a sheet, his father revealed a four-wheel all-terrain vehicle. "Happy birthday, bud," he said.

Tyler stared at it. "This is for me? For real?"

"Yup."

Sure, the thing looked a little beat up. But it was red, with black stripes, and it was a vehicle. And there was a cool motorcycle type helmet that was red with a black visor. He couldn't wait to take it out for a spin.

"Thanks, Dad! This is so awesome! Can I take it out?"

His father glanced at his mother and cleared his throat. "Maybe just in the yard."

"Sweet!"

He and his father pushed the four-wheeler out to the backyard. Tyler strapped on the helmet and got on. Just before he revved up the engine, he heard his mother say to his father, "Nice. Are you rewarding him for getting drunk?"

The ATV leapt forward, and now he couldn't hear their argument. He was flying. It was so much better than any video game. He spun out, did some donuts, then stopped. "Hey Sam, want a ride?"

Sam ran into the garage and dug up a bike helmet. "Don't go too fast," she warned, then sat behind him and held him tight around his waist.

For fun, he did a three sixty. She shrieked, but he could tell she was having fun. Sam had always liked stuff like that, roller coasters and horror movies. By the time he dropped Sam off, his mother had gone inside.

Sam had made plans to go out with her friends, but while she was getting ready, Tyler wandered into her room and sat on her bed.

"What's up," Sam asked. She was cross-legged on the floor, putting on her make up in the full length mirror attached to her closet door.

"I was thinking... you know that movie we were watching last night? 'The Changeling'?"

"Yeah?"

"Remember that part where the psychic lady was doing automatic writing? I thought maybe you had some books about it." Sam had a lot of books about occult stuff. Most of them were old, bought at used book stores.

"Why do you want to know about that?" Sam asked. She got up and started looking through her bookshelves.

"Well, you have to keep this a secret." Tyler took a deep breath. "See, I found this house in the woods, and I think it's haunted."

"Really? Where?"

Tyler explained the whole story of how he found the house, and how he felt when he entered the black hole room, and especially all about Danny and the basement and Tyler's dreams. "Now Danny wants to go back there, but it's really freaky. I'm thinking that if I can find out what the ghost wants, then it won't be so scary."

"It's like a real live horror movie, huh?"

Sam held an old paperback book out to him, titled, Contacting Spirits.

"So, have you read that book?" Tyler asked.

"This? Yeah. I don't know if it'll help you learn to do it. Basically you have to 'clear you mind' and 'keep your hand moving' and that's about it. Doing the scribbles like the lady in the movie helps you get used to keeping your hand moving. That's all there is to it. I got bored halfway through the book, and so I never actually gave it a try. But it sounds like you have a real ghost, so it might work better."

"Okay," Tyler said.

"And—you totally have to bring me out there this weekend!" Sam smacked Tyler in the shoulder. "I can't believe you didn't tell me about this sooner! Do you think maybe tomorrow we can go? I even have my camera." Sam was taking a photography class. "I could totally do something cool for my next assignment out there."

"Well, technically, I'm grounded. I've been sneaking out there... but probably Mom and Dad would let me go somewhere with you! You're responsible."

"I was actually thinking we could use your new toy."

"My what?"

"Your four-wheeler. That would get us out there pretty fast, huh?"

"Sam, you're a genius!"

As Tyler lay in bed that night, hoping the nightmares would stay away, he heard his parents arguing in their bedroom. "...I basically got the thing for free, Helen. I paid for parts, that's it. I couldn't pass that up..."

"...it's still a pretty extravagant gift for a kid who's grounded. He's sliding right back into his old behaviors and you're giving him presents."

"It's his birthday!"

"And now my lawn is all torn up with tire tracks..."

Tyler balled his comforter up against his ears. He supposed it was only natural for parents to make you feel like you were ten years old again.

***

On Sunday his parents wanted Sam to go shopping with them so they could buy her some "necessities." They wanted Tyler to go with them.

"Do I have to?" he whined, trying not to sound whiney.

"You are grounded," his mother reminded him. "And if we were to leave you home alone, who knows what trouble you'd get yourself into."

Tyler grumbled as he got ready. He tried to remind himself that there was still Monday, but he didn't know what time Sam would be heading back to campus. He took his phone and the book about automatic writing, and tried to ignore everyone the whole trip.

After dinner it looked like everyone was sitting around watching TV. Tyler had just plugged in his new video game when Sam ran into his room and flopped onto his bed. "Wanna go to the haunted house now?" she asked, her eyes shining.

"Um..." Tyler glanced out the window. "It's getting kind of dark."

"Are you kidding? You're such a wuss."

Instead of trying to convince Sam he wasn't a wuss, he punched her shoulder, then she punched him back, and soon they were wrestling on the floor until Sam got him in a headlock. Tyler yelped, "Fine, fine! We'll go now!" and Sam released her grip.

"I guess the four-wheeler wouldn't be too practical. We can take my car," Sam said. "I'll go grab some flashlights and my camera and tell Mom and Dad that we're going to hang out at Summer's house." Summer's little brother Brendan, who was a grade younger than Tyler, usually had some good video games.

"I have to call Danny. He needs to get his cell phone, remember?"

"Fine, whatever."

Less than ten minutes later, Sam and Tyler had picked up Danny at his house and were heading up Pine Hill Road. Tyler had his eyes peeled for the hidden drive sign, but saw something else instead.

"Pull over," he told Sam.

"Do you know who that is?" Sam asked.

"I think so."

Sam had barely stopped the car before Tyler was out.

"Karin?" he called.

The headlights shone on her back, making her blond hair and white dress jump out of the twilight. "Stop calling me that name!" she yelled, not turning around.

Tyler started running. She heard him coming and tried to run, but he was much quicker. He knew she could run as fast as him, but it almost looked like she wasn't trying. He caught her by the arm and turned her to face him. "Ellen?" he said.

She looked almost exactly like the drawings in his sketchbook. He could see Karin's face there, too, but ghostly, like it was behind a mask.

She wrapped her arms around him. "Tyler! I'm so glad it's you. No one else seems to know who I am."

The difference between Karin and Ellen was almost imperceptible. Ellen seemed more fragile, somehow, weaker. He wanted to scoop her up and hold her so she wouldn't break.

"I want to go home," she said into his chest.

"That's where we're going. Come on." He led her to Sam's car and sat in the backseat with her. "It's only a little further," he told Sam. Sam raised her eyebrows but said nothing about the girl Tyler had picked up on the side of the road.

Sam pulled over after the hidden drive sign on Pine Hill Road and they all got out. Sam, Danny, and Tyler all carried flashlights, and Tyler gave his notebook and pen to Sam so he could hold Karin's hand.

"It'll be better having more people," Danny said as they walked up the overgrown road. "That way, someone can hold the door open while we go into the basement, so it doesn't get stuck again."

"The basement?" Karin said, her voice wispy.

"We?" Tyler said. "You think I'm going back down there?"

"Come on, Ty," Danny whined.

Karin's voice was quiet and husky amid the crickets. "You can't go into the basement. No, she won't like that."

"Creepy," Sam said in her usual sarcastic way.

"She? Who is she?" Danny asked.

Karin didn't answer, but she did squeeze Tyler's hand a little tighter.

It was a much different atmosphere than the night Tyler had come here with Danny and Max and Max's friends. No one spoke, and everyone was jumping at the little sounds of the forest. As they got closer to the house, they walked in a tight huddle.

The front door was still open. The sight gave Tyler pause. He thought he had shut it. He remembered thinking about how something would escape from the house.

Looking at Karin, he wondered if something already had.

No one seemed to want to go inside first. They stood there, looking at the open door, looking up at the crumbling paint and broken windows.

Finally Sam said, "You're all a bunch of wusses," and barged into the kitchen.

Danny and Tyler sheepishly followed. Tyler pulled Karin along behind him. She went along with him willingly enough.

The basement door was open.

"Wasn't that door closed when you and I were here the other day?" Tyler asked Karin.

She shrugged, her eyes vacant.

He was pretty sure it had been closed. The sight of it open felt wrong. Like the house was inviting him and Danny down into the basement. Pulling them down.

"Okay, so Sam, you hold the door open," Danny said. "And Tyler and me will go down. Don't let that door shut, okay?"

Sam leaned against the door. She started pulling things out of her backpack: a tripod, her camera, different attachments. Danny watched her for a second, as if deciding whether she was really focused on keeping the door open, then headed into the black hole.

Tyler moved to go down with him, and Karin's hand slipped from his.

His flashlight illuminated the back of Danny's flannel shirt and the stone walls. He kept one hand on the wall for balance. Now, with the flashlight, he could see everything he hadn't been able to see before. Only a few steps down, giant spider webs stretched across the ceiling. Scurrying black shapes evaded his flashlight beam. The wood overhead looked rotten behind the silvery threads, but further down the webs were too thick to see the ceiling. Tyler forced his eyes down on the stairs.

"How far down did I fall?" Danny asked. "These stairs seem to go down really far..."

Tyler peered over Danny's shoulder. He couldn't see the bottom. Danny's flashlight beam seemed unable to penetrate the darkness more than a couple of feet. Tyler swallowed and looked back up at the door. Sam was still there, her flashlight resting on the counter.

She had a tripod set up, and she was focusing her camera down the stairwell.

It seemed like a black patch of nothing separated Danny and Tyler from Sam and the top of the stairs.

The coldness started to seep into his bones. He started shivering, and soon had to pull his hand away from the wall. The spider webs had started to spread across the surface like a sticky tapestry.

Loud clicks came from the top of the stairs – the shutter release on Sam's old camera.

"Oh, we're at the bottom. There it is!" Danny said. The beam from his flashlight dipped as he reached down to pick up Max's cell phone. "Damn! Thirty-four missed calls? I wonder if any are from Jasmine." The blue light and beeping from the phone seemed loud and unnatural. Tyler felt the stairs shift under his feet.

"Okay, let's go back then." Tyler turned to head upstairs.

"Come on, let's see what else is down here." Danny pointed his light into the basement.

"What is wrong with you?" Tyler gasped. He was having a hard time breathing. "Don't you remember all your nightmares or anything?"

"I need to look. I need to make sure this is a regular old basement. Hey, look at this!" Danny moved away into the pitch-black room.

Tyler hurried after him, and grabbed his shirt. "Come on, Danny, this isn't funny." Tyler felt like he finally understood the phrase "sweating bullets." The collar of his t-shirt was already soaked, and he could feel huge drops worming their way down his jaw line and neck.

"Do you see that?" Danny shone the flashlight beam on a pile of debris in the nearly empty basement. "Do you see that?"

"It's just a pile of junk," Tyler said. He yanked on Danny's shirt. "Come on, please. Let's go upstairs. Where it's warm."

"No, no, do you see?"

Danny stepped closer, pulling Tyler with him. Tyler shone his flashlight on the pile.

In the doubled light, white objects among the debris looked disturbingly like bones.

"Are those...?"

"No!" Tyler yelled. The sound reverberated in the stone basement. "Please, don't touch them." He watched Danny reach his hand forward. He was going to be sick.

"Stop it!" Tyler said.

He couldn't watch anymore. He turned and ran toward the stairs. He could hear a horrible dry clacking behind him. Where were the stairs? Tyler swung his flashlight around. All he could see were giant blocks of stone.

"Look at me, Tyler, look at me," Danny whispered behind him.

Tyler whipped around and came face to face with a skull.

Danny laughed as Tyler staggered backwards.

When Tyler's hands touched the cold stone behind him, darkness pulsed in for a moment, then the stones that formed the basement walls began to exude a silvery gray light. In that strange light he could see a shape, a foggy person-shape drifting. It was hovering near where

Danny had been standing. Tyler moved forward to warn Danny, and the image disappeared. Danny's flashlight beam nearly blinded him.

"Come on, it's just a skull. It's not like there are maggots crawling over it or anything."

"Get that thing away from me," Tyler wheezed.

"Fine, fine, whatever." Danny tucked it under his arm and headed off into the darkness.

"Wait!" Tyler called, and reattached himself to Danny's shirt. Danny found the stairs out of the basement with no problem.

Back in the kitchen, Tyler collapsed on the floor. He used his sleeve to wipe away the sweat on his face.

"Hey, Sam, check this out."

"Awesome! This was down there?"

"Yeah, there was this pile of all like dirt and bones and stuff."

"Look how the skull is cracked back here. I bet this person was murdered by a blow to the head."

"I think you've been watching too many of those forensics shows on TV," Tyler said.

Sam gave him a look then said to Danny, "Here, put it on the counter. I want to take a picture of it. I'm going to have the best photography project ever."

It wasn't until Sam had placed the skull just so on the counter and done a test with her light meter and taken a couple of shots that Tyler suddenly realized someone was missing. "Where's Karin?" he asked.

Danny spun in a circle and shrugged.

"Sam?" Sam focused on the skull, but Tyler could see her cheeks were red. "I don't know. I wasn't really paying attention..."

"Great," Tyler muttered, hauling himself to his feet.

"What, like I'm supposed to baby-sit all of you?" Sam snapped. "She probably just wanted to explore upstairs or something."

"Whatever. I'll go find her."

Tyler stalked into the living room. And stopped dead in his tracks.

Chapter 20

Karin was there, seated on one of the milk crates.

Tyler didn't know what to say, so he didn't say anything. He sat down on the other milk crate and set his flashlight on the floor, beam up, so it acted as a weird lamp. His fingers danced over the water-soaked cards.

Now that he could see her, he saw that she wasn't wearing a white dress like he'd thought. It was a nightgown. What was Karin doing in a nightgown at seven o'clock at night? He couldn't imagine what had been going on at Karin's house the past couple of days. If Karin was actually Ellen, her parents must have been freaking out. He wondered if they had brought her to a doctor, thinking she had some kind of amnesia.

"Helloooo..."

Tyler whipped his head around. Danny had the skull stuck on his fist and was making it talk like a puppet. "Knock it off!" Tyler yelled.

"Geez, touchy," Danny said. He stepped into the living room and yanked the skull off his fist. The bone went flying across the floor.

The moment the skull touched the floor, a loud crash shook the house.

Sam ran into the living room, clutching her camera to her chest. "What was that?"

"It sounded too loud to be this skull here." Danny walked over and kicked the skull with the toe of his untied boots. It rolled and bumped across the floor.

"It sounded like it came from upstairs," Sam said.

They all slowly turned their eyes to look up at the ceiling.

"Maybe it was thunder," Danny said.

Tyler didn't say anything. He looked at Karin. She was staring straight ahead, her eyes wide and blank.

Long minutes passed and nothing happened. Sam laughed nervously. "I guess it's nothing."

"Yeah," Danny agreed. "I got Max's cell phone, we can go now if you want, Tyler."

"Good idea." Tyler stood.

"Wait, you have to try that automatic writing thing," Sam said. "I'll go get your notebook."

"Automatic writing? What's that?" Danny asked.

"We saw it in this movie. You let your hand go and any ghosts that are around will write a message," Sam explained. She returned to the living room and looked around. Finally she put the notebook on the makeshift table, on top of the cards. Tyler sank back down to sit.

"Do we need to hold hands or something?" Sam picked up Karin's limp hand, then dropped it. "Wow. Your hands are freezing!"

Karin stared blankly.

Sam looked at her, then continued. "Well, we should all close our eyes or something. Here's the pen, Tyler. Okay, now start scribbling." Tyler moved the pen in circles. "Loosen your grip. Okay." Sam shut her eyes. Danny did the same. Tyler swallowed, and closed his eyes too. "Spiiiiirits.... Spiiiiiiirits who live in this hoooouse..." Sam's intonation sounded as cheesy as the movie, yet no one was laughing. "Come to us, spiiiiiiirits... we wish to knooooow why you haunt this plaaaaaace..."

Sam peeked out of one eye. "Anything?" she whispered.

Tyler shook his head.

She closed her eyes. "Spiiiiiiirits... why are you here? Why do you not find peeeeace?"

"This isn't going to work." Tyler threw down the pen.

"You have to give it a chance," Sam said.

"Maybe she should do it." Danny jerked his thumb at Karin. "She looks like she's in a trance or whatever."

They exchanged glances. Tyler picked up the pen and placed it in Karin's right hand.

"Close your eyes," Sam instructed. "Spiiiiiiirits... where are you?"

"I don't think you need to talk in that stupid voice," Tyler said.

"Look!"

Karin's hand was moving in a jerky line.

"What does it say?" Danny asked.

Sam read aloud, " 'We have always been here.' "

As they watched, breathless in silence, Karin's hand continued across the page.

"We will always be here," her hand wrote.

"Are you for real?" Danny said, a shriek coming into his voice.

"Whoooo aaaare yooooou?" Sam asked the darkness in her best séance voice.

"Our name is Legion, for we are many," Karin's hand scribbled.

"What?" Danny said.

Sam snatched the paper out from under Karin's still-moving pen and stared at it. Then she stood up and threw the paper on the table. "It's from the Bible. The Book of Revelations, about the coming of the Antichrist," Sam said. "It was in the movie 'The Omen.' Nice try, Tyler."

"What?" Tyler asked.

"Like you haven't ever seen that movie. I have it in my room."

"I've never watched that movie!" Tyler said.

"Liar!"

Just then, an ominous creak came from upstairs.

"You guys heard that, right?" Danny asked, clutching his flashlight to his chest.

The floorboards overhead began creaking. Dust sprinkled down from the ceiling.

"Who's up there?" Sam's voice sounded a bit unhinged. She whirled on Tyler. "Is this all some stupid joke?"

"I don't know what that is! It's what I told you before!"

"There is no such thing as ghosts!" Sam screamed at him.

Behind Sam, Karin rose, still staring forward.

"Please, Sam," Tyler said, feeling wetness on his face. "I don't know what that is. I never lied to you."

"You're a liar! There are no ghosts! You made it up! You got one of your stupid friends to go upstairs and make weird noises to freak me out. Admit it!"

"It's real, Sam! I swear!"

Karin moved forward. The footsteps upstairs had reached the end of the hallway.

"I think we should go." Danny shifted from foot to foot. "Like, now."

"Good idea," said Tyler.

"No way," said Sam. She grabbed her camera and stuck it in Tyler's face. "I'm going to prove that you're a liar."

Tyler watched as Sam stalked past Karin and started up the stairs. "Here I come," Sam shouted up the stairwell.

She took a few shots along the way, smirking at Tyler with each snap of the shutter. She made it most of the way up, before she stopped dead and lowered the camera from her face. For a moment Sam stood with her mouth open, then backed up, seeming to forget that she was on stairs, stumbling backwards and sliding down a couple of stairs, her back against the wall. Then she got control of her feet and started running.

"What's up there?" Danny asked her as she flew past them. "What did you see?" This last question he nearly screamed, since she was already tossing her camera equipment in her bag and running out of the house.

Karin was now ascending the stairs, moving slowly, as if in a dream.

"Come on, Tyler, we gotta get out of here." Danny tugged on Tyler's sleeve.

"What about Karin?"

Danny hesitated, looking at Karin, looking at the door. Then he finally bolted for the door. His voice echoed in his wake. "Sorry, man!"

Tyler stood there, his lone flashlight beam lighting the darkness.

"Karin, stop," Tyler said.

Karin was almost at the top of the stairs now.

"Ellen?" he tried.

At the name, Karin stopped and looked down at him. "I have to go, Tyler. Please come with me."

She smiled so sweetly, Tyler forgot about the other presence at the top of the stairs. He walked up, and put his hand in the one she held out for him. She led him to the second floor.

Karin moved through the darkness with phosphorescence, exuding her halo. Tyler switched off his flashlight. She was so beautiful. All that silvery blond hair, those pure blue eyes. He would follow her anywhere. She could be his religion.

She walked past Ellen's bedroom, to the door of the little room. The black hole room. As she laid her hand on the doorknob, she smiled at him, then opened the door.

It wasn't so bad in the room with Karin at his side. Tyler felt her presence warming him, keeping him grounded. What had he been so afraid of? She moved him in front of the bed and pushed his chest until he sat down. His smile widened. Karin, he meant to say, but instead he said, "Ellen."

She smiled down at him. There were straps attached to the bed frame, why hadn't he noticed that before? She pushed on his chest more. She wanted him to lie down. He did what she wanted. The heat of her touch, the smile playing on her lips, he knew what she wanted.

She moved her hands to the collar of her nightgown, unbuttoned the first button. He could only gaze up at her. But as she moved to the second button, he realized that he was getting cold. Fast. His breath was clouding up. The light that had seemed to come from Karin's purity dimmed. He couldn't make out her face distinctly anymore. There was no moon, and the shadows warped Karin's face into something else.

She moved to the third button.

Suddenly Tyler needed to get up. He tried to sit up, but it felt like a huge weight sat on his chest. He couldn't breathe so well, either. The cloud of breath in front of his face grew smaller and smaller with each exhalation. The shadows on Karin's face seemed to dance, to move in ways that shadows shouldn't move across someone's face. One second her eye seemed to be in the middle of her cheek, the next it had slid back to her ear, replaced by her mouth.

Her hands slipped down to the fourth button.

Tyler scrambled for something, anything, to pull himself up. He tried to grip the edges of the mattress, his feet sliding around uselessly.

She leaned over him. Her hair felt like spider webs grazing his cheeks. He did not want to kiss this thing. He turned his head away, squeezing his eyes shut.

"Don't you want to join us, Tyler?" Ellen asked. It wasn't Karin's voice, he knew that much. It sounded like a young girl's voice, but behind it he heard something else, a rotting kind of wetness. "You can stay here forever, with me."

Tyler shook his head.

"That... makes me very sad..."

Abruptly Tyler felt her presence fade. He felt a moment of relief—the weight lifted from his chest, warmth returned to his body with the pinpricks of circulation he normally felt when his leg had fallen asleep.

Then darkness crushed him.

Chapter 21

"Papa? Are you feeling okay?" Ellen asked her father. She was carrying a suitcase into the house. Her father stood staring up at the ceiling.

He didn't answer, so she looked up at the ceiling. A water stain had seeped out from a corner of the living room.

"Ellen, dear, please go put your things away," her mother said behind her. "Your father is very busy with important matters."

"Yes, Mother," Ellen said.

She clattered up the stairs lugging her suitcase. When she entered her new room, she hopped up and down. Her father had made this vanity for her, she knew—she'd watched him work on it in his workshop in the city. It was perfect. He had painted it, too. She ran her fingers over the tiny flowers twining their way around the surface. She looked at herself in the mirror, striking a pose like the glamorous women in her mother's magazines. She imagined herself one day applying makeup and powder and curling her hair back into a fancy chignon.

She could hardly believe her father had built this whole house. A few weeks ago, out of the blue, her father had come home from work and announced that the logging company he worked for had gone out of business a year earlier, and he had been working on building a house for them all to live in.

Ellen flopped down on her bed, which her mother had already made up with Ellen's favorite quilt. She didn't like to think about how her parents had argued after that announcement. "What money have we been living on, if you haven't been getting paid?" her mother had demanded immediately. From her bedroom, where she'd been sent, Ellen pressed her ear to the wall and still couldn't hear her father's answer. "My inheritance? You've been spending my inheritance? That money was meant for Ellen! How could you? You do realize that the country is in the midst of a Depression?"

Somehow, in the weeks following, her father had convinced her mother about the new house. This was Ellen's first time here, but her parents had been going there every day while Ellen went to school or for treatments. Ellen hated the treatments, but her mother had been convinced they would work for her condition. Now that they had moved into the new house, however, her mother had told her she didn't need to go for treatments anymore.

This new house was wonderful.

The next day at breakfast Ellen's mother suggested that she invite her best friend Lily over for a play date. "Tell her she can sleep over, too," Ellen's mother suggested.

"Can I ring her on the telephone right now?" Ellen asked.

Her mother nodded. Ellen rushed to the telephone and dialed the operator, who connected her to Lily's house. She was hopping up and down with excitement. It wasn't every day that she was allowed to have a friend over, never mind overnight. Lily agreed to come over. She said her father would drive her over after lunch.

"Where will Lily sleep?" Ellen asked her mother after hanging up the telephone.

"Oh, your father has prepared a spare room," her mother said.

"A spare room? Can I see?"

"Oh, no," her mother said quickly. "Not yet." She smiled down at Ellen.

"All right." Ellen supposed her father might have a bit more work to do on the room before it was ready. She decided to go up to her room and lay down. She always felt so tired these days, and she would need her rest in order to properly entertain her friend later.

That night, at bedtime, Lily went to bed in the spare room, while Ellen went into her own bedroom. She felt exhausted. Lily had ruddy cheeks that complimented her auburn hair and a bubbly personality to match. Ellen had tried to keep up with her friend, even as they were only playing cards downstairs by the fireplace (Ellen was always so cold), but by seven-thirty she had nearly collapsed.

"Ellen, dear, I believe it's time for bed," her mother had said.

Ellen could tell Lily was disappointed. Most girls their age went to bed later, Ellen knew from listening to gossip at school. But Lily hadn't mentioned that it was too early for bedtime. Lily was such a kind girl.

While Lily went up to the spare room to change into her pajamas, Ellen's father had carried her up the stairs. Her mother had helped her into her nightgown and tucked her into bed.

"See you in the morning," Lily said at Ellen's door.

"Good night," Ellen said. In the darkness she lay awake—it always happened this way, with her body drained but her mind still sharp. She heard her parents walking around, doors opening and closing. She heard a low moaning sound that came again and again. She still hadn't seen the spare room, and she tried to imagine what it looked like. There was probably a bed with a canopy, like the one in the Sears catalog Ellen had admired so much. Hopefully Lily would tell the girls at school how wonderful Ellen's new house was, so they would all be jealous.

Soon after that, Ellen fell into a deep, heavy sleep.

When she woke up, light streamed in through her bedroom windows. She felt better than she'd felt in years, since the doctor had diagnosed her. She stretched and hopped out of bed. She threw on her slippers and her robe and ran down the hall to the spare room.

The doorknob seemed stuck.

"Lily? Lily, time to wake up!" Ellen called, jiggling the knob.

She thought she heard that low moaning again. She leaned her ear against the door.

"Ellen!"

She jumped at the sound of her own name. "Mother! I was trying to get Lily up. I didn't realize I'd slept so late!"

"You slept very late indeed," her mother said, steering her by her shoulders away from the spare room. "You took ill, and have been in bed for two weeks."

"Really?" Ellen tried to remember. "I must have been very sick."

"Yes, a high fever, delirium... but you look much better this morning."

Ellen went back to her room to get changed, but first sat and looked at herself in her vanity mirror. She touched her face, the skin on her cheeks, under her eyes. Where before her cheeks had sunken in from the wasting disease's effects, they were full and even had a rosy blush to them. Where previously there had been dark circles under her eyes from her poor health and difficulty sleeping, there were none. Her eyes looked clear and bright blue.

Even though Ellen felt much better, her parents wouldn't allow her to return to school. After the first few days, it didn't bother Ellen so much. She enjoyed drawing and painting and reading, sometimes going on hikes into the forest with her father. Her mother started a garden, and soon the family didn't leave except for occasional trips to the bank or the grocery. Her parents didn't keep a calendar, but somehow they knew when Christmas was, and Ellen's birthday. Ellen saw the seasons changing, but soon even they started to blur together.

Slowly she began to notice how her parents' hair had begun to turn gray. Yet Ellen's reflection in the mirror remained the same.

One Christmas, Ellen opened a package containing a silver handled hairbrush and mirror set wrapped in newspaper. She caught a glimpse of the date, 1952, before her father whisked it away.

For a time Ellen thought the date she'd seen must have been a mistake. How could it be possible? She didn't want to believe it. The trees outside looked the same as always, bare in winter, budding in spring, and cloaked in bright colors in fall. Nothing else in her world had changed. She read her books. She sometimes drew portraits of her parents. There seemed to be more lines on their faces now.

Then one day, her mother died.

It was an accident. Her mother had gone into the basement to get a jar of preserves, nothing out of the ordinary. Her parents rarely went into the basement. In fact, they'd put a large lock on the door to keep Ellen out. "The stairs are dangerous," they told her. She didn't mind, she was a good girl. And she'd felt that icy cold wind coming up from down there. That wind cut right through her bones.

Her father was out splitting wood. Ellen was in the living room, reading, when she heard her mother gasp, and the rolling series of cracks and crashes. Her father had come running in immediately, meeting Ellen at the doorway.

"Mother?" Ellen called down into the darkness.

"Ellen, go upstairs," her father had said. He lit a kerosene lamp and prepared to go down. The lamp shook in his hand. Ellen realized that his hand shook not because he was afraid, but because he was old and feeble. She had to stay. What if he fell, too? She would have to call for the police or an ambulance.

She saw the light go down and down, grow smaller and smaller. "Ellen, go upstairs!" her father barked again.

"Yes, sir," she murmured, and went up to her room.

It felt like hours later that her father came into her room. His boots were caked in red clayey dirt. There were smears of blood on his shirt and pants, and tufts of his gray hair stood on end. "Your mother is dead," he said.

There was no funeral. Ellen knew deep down that her family was entirely isolated now. There was no one to carry her mother's body out of the basement. Her father was too old, and Ellen was too small. Her father simply locked the cellar door and neither of them spoke of it again. Life went on as before. Six months later, Ellen found her father's body in bed after he didn't wake up one morning.

Ellen wasn't sure what to do. She picked up the telephone, but there was no operator there, just a buzzing sound. She thought about burying her father. She simply could not leave him there in bed. She'd had enough nightmares about her mother down in the basement. She even dug a hole in the yard. She was able to drag her father's body out of bed, down the stairs, and into the kitchen. Then she realized that she had dug his grave on the slope. She would have to drag him out of the front door, then around back, and up a hill. At that point she collapsed and began to cry. Her father's body was already banged up from going down the stairs.

The basement door loomed in front of her.

Her mother was still down there. Perhaps it would be best for her father to lie in rest beside her.

The keys to the lock were in her father's room. It was a simple matter to unlock the door and push his body over the doorstop. Gravity and the steepness of the stairs took care of the rest. She locked the basement door and left the keys on the counter.

For the first time in her life, Ellen was entirely alone. The house moaned. She took a bath, tried to scrub the dirt out of her pores. She rubbed her skin raw and still felt unclean. For the rest of the day she lay on her bed reading.

Over the next few days, the loneliness was so present it felt like another person lurking in the house with her. She cooked food for herself, tried to ignore the moaning that seemed to come out of the floorboards and the walls. At night it got worse. Wind seemed to attack the house, wailing and shrieking. Ellen huddled under her blankets, her head under her pillow to muffle the sound.

Inexplicably, Ellen's illness seemed to return. She felt weak, insubstantial. She lay down most days. One day she looked in the mirror and was startled to see her reflection. To see through her reflection. She looked down at her hands. They still appeared solid, but they felt hollow and airy. She went out into the hallway to go down to the kitchen, and only realized a moment later that her door was closed behind her without her having closed it. She had passed through the door.

Years passed. Ellen never felt the need to eat. She never slept. She didn't know what year it was.

Once, some men came into the house, and took the living room furniture. They left the kitchen door open behind them.

Another time, three teenage boys stood outside of the house and shot at the window panes with a B-B gun.

Occasionally, men would come in alone or with a bottle for company and pass the night.

One day, a woman came to the house.

Ellen sensed her presence and floated down. The woman peered through the window panes. She walked around the perimeter of the house. Then she left.

Ellen waited by the window. It was her first visitor in years, the first marker of time passing. From the style of the woman's clothes, trousers and a wide-lapelled blazer, Ellen could see things had changed. She had never been allowed to wear trousers.

Eventually, the woman did return. She brought trash bags and a young girl about Ellen's age. "Mom, can I look around?" the girl asked once they were inside.

"That's fine, April, but don't touch anything," the woman said.

The woman proceeded to open the cupboards, but most of the food had been taken by the overnight guests. Things like the toaster and the telephone had been taken, too. The woman started picking up the trash left around by the various other guests, as well as the leaves and debris that had begun collecting in the corners.

Ellen grew bored watching the woman clean. She went upstairs and found the girl April sitting at her vanity. Sometime over the years, the mirror had cracked. Her once beautiful bedroom was trashed. April quickly became bored when she found nothing in the vanity, and went to explore the other rooms. She opened the door to Ellen's parents' room, but Ellen pushed the girl out. She didn't want anyone in her parents' room.

Next, April went to the spare room.

All of Ellen's life, that door had been locked. Sometimes her mother or father had gone in, and usually they had been secretive about it. They had forbidden Ellen to go in there, and eventually Ellen had forgotten all about it. Now Ellen looked over April's shoulder.

Ellen had barely gotten a peek inside, at the small bed and the small table with the Bible, had seen someone lying in the bed, when April screamed and tried to slam the door.

Ellen stuck out her hand and held the door open. She realized that she had just walked through April, and suddenly her grip on the door released.

She was trapped in the dark room. Ellen moved closer to the shape in the bed. She hadn't had a problem seeing in the dark in years.

The shape in the bed consisted of bones and dust, and what looked like a wig. A wig of gray, old hair. Small details suddenly stabbed her eyes: the print of the dress covering the bones, the straps on the bed, the fact that the book she'd assumed was a Bible had a gilded cross on the cover that was upside down.

Behind the closed door, Ellen heard April screaming for her mother. The screams continued for long minutes, as Ellen slowly came to the realization that this body had once belonged to her friend Lily. Lily, who had been trapped here since that night, kept alive by her parents for some sick reason, who had died only because Ellen hadn't known that Lily was in this room.

"I've been waiting for you to come and help me, Ellen," said a voice behind her. "I knew you would come."

Chapter 22

Tyler woke screaming, feeling bits of bone and dust and hair beneath him. In the pure black darkness, he crashed out of the bed, stumbled around the tiny room, his hands finding only walls every direction he turned. His knees bumped the nightstand. He grabbed the table to keep himself from falling, and his hand found the book. The book he'd thought was a Bible, too. He picked it up and stuck it into the waistband of his jeans. Slowly, he turned around in place. He should be facing the door now.

His hand found the knob and opened the door.

Total silence greeted him.

Tyler stepped into the hallway cautiously. His shirt was soaked in sweat, and the sudden drop in temperature made him shiver. The darkness was faintly illuminated by the moon through the hole in the roof. Tyler stood there, listening, and heard nothing.

"Karin?" he called.

Nothing... then faintly he heard a voice, someone far away, calling.

"Karin? Is that you?" he asked. He moved down the hall, down the stairs, wincing every time the steps squealed beneath his sneakers. "Karin?" In the middle of the living room he stopped and listened again. The voice was slightly louder.

Of course. Where else would she be but in the basement?

Tyler took a deep breath and moved to the doorway of the cellar.

An icy cold wind blew the hair straight off of his forehead. The darkness was absolute. He needed some kind of light. Sam had taken most of her photo equipment with her, but it looked like she had missed a few things in her hurry, little mechanical odds and ends and boxes containing film and tiny batteries. A gleam of orange caught his eye. He pulled out the tube.

It was his lighter.

He thumbed the flint. The little flame that popped up mesmerized him, but it wouldn't do anything to light up that enormous darkness in the basement. He needed something bigger.

He remembered the broom in the closet. When he yanked open the door, the broom handle fell toward him and he jumped back, his heart pounding. "Get yourself together," he muttered as he inspected the straw end of the broom. Nice and dry, as he had expected. He held the lighter under the bristles. The little flame caught almost instantly. He tucked the lighter in his jeans pocket and returned to the basement door.

He started down the stairs. Almost immediately, the ropes of spider webs over his head burned away. Bits of gossamer fell like ashes against his face and shoulders. He pulled his t-shirt up over his nose to avoid inhaling the ash and the little charred spider corpses. The smoke from the broom torch stung his eyes. He didn't have too long—the broom was so old and dry that it was burning fast. His feet hurried down the stairs, almost recklessly.

The stairs ended and Tyler slowed. He could see other lights ahead. Dozens of candles, placed around the basement.

In the center stood Karin. Or was she truly Ellen now?

Tyler pulled the t-shirt away from his face and stared at her. Pieces of his torch were burning off onto the ground. The same blond hair, the same rosy skin. "Karin?" he tried.

"No, Tyler," said Ellen's voice, rasping from Karin's throat. Her blue eyes winked in the flickering light. "Didn't you see?"

"Where is Karin?" Tyler asked. He remembered all too clearly the image of the bones lying in that bed where he had lain.

"She is me now. Don't you know that?"

"But she... you only lived on because of your friend Lily, right? You took Lily's life, but she was still there, in the house."

Ellen looked at him kindly. "That was the only way my parents knew how to do it," she said. "They... didn't understand."

"Understand what?"

"They thought they needed to kill me first," she stated. "And then they performed the ritual so that my body stayed... alive. It's very ineffective. My real body rotted away a long time ago."

Tyler shuddered.

"But Lily told me of a better way."

"Lily told you?"

"That was how April became me. I simply take over. The stones make me strong enough."

The newspaper article had said that April—or the girl he assumed had been April, who had wandered out of the forest in 1971 claiming to be Ellen Birdsall—had been sent to a mental hospital. "What happened to April?"

"I—we, I suppose I should say—were sent to an asylum. You already know that, I can see. I was not afraid, but these doctors were able to perform a sort of exorcism, using electricity. It became intolerable to be in her body, and so I left, and returned here to wait."

It took Tyler a few minutes to grasp what she meant by an electrical exorcism—shock treatments. He felt relieved that April was now okay, or at least not possessed by a ghost, but his fear returned quickly enough.

"But how could Lily tell you that, if she was dead... if she had died before?"

Ellen laughed, a sound that bounced off the stones and multiplied. A cackling haunted echo. "She's my best friend, Tyler. Lily lives in the stones. She whispers to me. She wants to help me, so I can help her. Isn't that what friends do?"

The black shoes. Tyler could see the black shoes on the edges of the darkness. Instinctively he started to back away. "Ellen, please... how can I... Karin..." He couldn't take his eyes off of those shoes now that he'd found them. He licked his lips.

Ellen took a step toward him. "Will you stay with me forever?"

"I... I can't," he said.

"You can!" A pleading tone came into her voice. "You love me, don't you? I know you do. All those days you came here, simply to be near me, reading the books I love, simply to know me better. You loved me from the moment you heard my name, that day in the cemetery."

"The cemetery!" Tyler said. "Aren't you buried there? You died when you were fourteen. You're dead and buried. This isn't real."

"Oh, but it is." Ellen glided closer to him, the hem of her nightgown floating along with her. "No one is buried in that coffin. You know that; it was part of the story you told to Karin."

She moved closer. Tyler found that he couldn't move away.

"Tyler," she whispered. She caressed his cheek with a warm hand. "If you can't stay here, you need to bring that other girl back. Ever since you first came here, we've been waiting for someone more... suitable... to come along. You offered us Karin. Karin was perfect for me, but Lily wants the other girl that was here tonight."

"Sam? Lily wants Sam?"

"Sam? Is that her name? Is that short for Samantha?" A pause while all around them the house moaned. "Yes, Lily thinks that will work," Ellen stated.

"You can't have my sister! I won't let you!"

Ellen's caress turned into a chokehold. "If you won't bring her back here, Lily is willing to take you instead. She already used you once. She would prefer a female, but it really doesn't matter to her."

Tyler tried to scream no, but his words couldn't make it past those cold hands on his throat.

"You will bring her. You will escort her here before the full moon." Ellen leaned close, and Tyler could smell on her breath the stench of a corpse. "If you don't, we will come for her."

Her grip became menacingly tight, and he struggled against it. He couldn't breathe. His eyes rolled over to see those black shoes at the edge of the shadows, waiting for him. Then the shadows moved in and covered his eyes.

Chapter 23

He woke up in his own bed, pine needles and twigs stuck to his feet. Pulling himself into a sitting position, he tried to remember all that had happened. Sam and Danny abandoning him, and Karin...

Was Karin still in the house?

He gazed out his bedroom window, into the darkness barely visible in the moonlight.

Moonlight...

Before the full moon, Ellen had said. There was the moon, three-quarters full. He had less than a week.

***

Sam left early Monday morning, leaving Tyler's mother in an uproar.

"Why so early? I thought you'd at least be here for dinner!"

"I've got a big paper due tomorrow, and I need to make sure it's perfect," Sam said.

Their voices dug Tyler out from a heavy sleep.

"But we've barely spent any time with you!" his mother complained, then changed her tactic. "Why don't we take you out for lunch, and then head back? You'll have plenty of time for your paper. I know you love the Olive Garden."

"Thanks, but I'm not real hungry."

Tyler rolled over, feeling a hard something cutting into his stomach. Had he rescued another library book from the house? When he saw the upside down cross on the book's cover, he threw the book across the room. He knew why Sam was leaving.

And he was happy she was leaving.

At least, he felt happy until he remembered that if he couldn't bring Sam back to the house, Lily would take him instead.

He rolled over and buried his face in his pillow.

***

Karin wasn't in school on Tuesday. Tyler sat behind her empty seat in Algebra, gripping his pencil. She couldn't still be at that house, right?

All day yesterday he had studied that old book, trying to touch it as little as possible. The binding looked like it was made out of leather, but the pages didn't look like paper. They looked like... skin. At first he'd told himself it was parchment paper, but the texture of the paper wasn't dry and crumbly like parchment would have been after so many years. It was oily and soft. The book emanated a smell Tyler couldn't quite place, but it made the bile rise in his throat.

The words in the old book were in English, written in the strange style of the Colonial period where sometimes s looked like f and contained a lot of words Tyler had to look up. In the chapter with the heading "Daemon Possession," there was an inked drawing of a person strapped to a table or bed, emitting an eel-like black shape from his open mouth, his eyes rolled back in agony.

He couldn't quite understand if this was a daemon being exorcized, or if this was how the daemon entered the body. The idea of a person's soul looking so black and foul made Tyler feel sick.

In the dream he'd had lying on Lily's bed in the black hole room, Lily's living spirit had been put into Ellen's dead body. In the story he had told Karin, Ellen's dead spirit was put into Lily's living body.

The idea of having Lily's black, slimy spirit forced into his mouth actually made him vomit.

His mother had heard him throwing up, but after asking if he was okay, she demanded, "Were you out drinking again last night? I knew I couldn't count on you to keep your act together."

Tyler didn't answer her. He listened to his mother rant about how he was still grounded and how he needed to stop this behavior or they'd send him back to therapy. She said she knew he'd set a fire out in the woods a few nights ago. Finally, after getting no response from Tyler, she gave up on him.

He stayed in the bathroom, his cheek pressed against the cold porcelain, until he heard her footsteps fade away. Then he crept back to his room, where he slept for most of the day.

He hadn't been able to bring himself to look at the book since. His skin broke out in a cold sweat at the thought of touching it. It still occupied all of his thoughts. He looked down at his math notes and saw that he had sketched a good likeness to the drawing of the bed with its straps, empty and waiting for him.

The paper crumpled beneath his hand.

***

At dinner that night, he poked at his meal, scraping his fork against his plate to accentuate the tight silence beneath his parents' conversation about their workday. He could tell by the irritated line of his mother's lips that she thought he was playing sick. She couldn't even begin to imagine that he wasn't the Bad Kid who set a dumpster on fire.

Or a warehouse...

He slumped his shoulders and dropped his head so that his whole world consisted of a plate of dry chicken, a lump of mashed potatoes, and a few green beans.

Maybe he was a delinquent. There was no reason for him to have done any of it. No outer reason, anyway. He hadn't been abused or lived in poverty. Danny's family appeared in his mind, the ragged thin sisters, the parents that never seemed to be around.

Out from the vault of his memory came images from that period of time when he was in juvie... or what he liked to call juvie, to make it sound like he was tough.

The Riversedge Rehabilitation Center for Boys.

It sounded like some place where innocent boys who have been in horrible accidents go to get well.

Tyler had allowed those three months he spent at Riversedge to fade from his memory. Now, as he tasted the sourness of bile in his throat, he remembered the feel of threadbare carpet pressed against his face, the strong scent of bleach and urine pricked his nose. He heard the curses of the angry and the screams of the outraged. He felt his own throat screaming, his muscles wound up and ready to fight.

"May I be excused?" Without waiting for an answer, he dumped his dishes in the sink and ran upstairs to bed.

All week he remained on edge. He couldn't eat, he couldn't sleep—every creak of his house sent his body into high alert, thinking Lily had come for him. Every night the moon glared down its warning.

Before the full moon...

When Karin was in her seat in Algebra on Friday, her pen poised over her notebook like nothing had happened, Tyler stopped short in the doorway. A kid behind him slammed into his back and he stumbled into the classroom, still staring.

Had Lily sent Ellen after him, to check up on him? Tyler swallowed the hard lump in his throat. What would she do here, in front of everyone?

The bell rang.

Or maybe this was the real Karin. Maybe somehow he had imagined everything and Karin was back to normal.

"Mr. McCracken, please take your seat," Mr. Hill said sharply.

Karin looked up at him briefly. He saw the ice blue eyes and his stomach dropped.

He edged toward his seat, his eyes glued to Ellen.

"Today, Mr. McCracken."

Everyone was staring at him. He could feel their stares burning into his neck.

Mr. Hill started class and slowly their attention moved away. Under his desk Tyler clenched and unclenched his fists. Don't freak out. She can't do anything in school. Pretend everything's normal. Pretend.

Part of normal would be flirting with Karin. Talking to her. Walking out of class with her and through the hallways, holding her hand.

Can't do it. I can't touch that thing.

No, he shouldn't feel that way. It was still Karin's body. He could still get Ellen out of Karin's body somehow. Maybe the book showed a way. He could try reading the book again.

I don't want to touch that thing, either.

The class period passed minute by agonizing minute. The smell of Karin's—Ellen's—lavender shampoo clogged his nose and made him want to gag. It smelled like death.

When the bell signaled the end of class, Tyler was ready. He bolted for the door like he was running the hundred yard dash.

"Hold up just a minute, Mr. McCracken."

Tyler halted. His shoulders stiff, he turned to his teacher.

"Yes?"

"You seem to be having some difficulty concentrating in class," Mr. Hill began. "Yet your grades are very good."

Out of the corner of his eye, Tyler watched Karin drift out of the room. He relaxed a bit. "Um, thank you?"

Mr. Hill appraised Tyler with a hand on his hip. "I have a difficult time believing that you are getting these grades without extra help."

"Karin was helping me a little. And one of my other friends who's really good at math." What was the guy getting at? he wondered.

"Helping you how?"

Suddenly it fell into place, and Tyler's body reacted immediately. His pulse raced, his breathing quickened, his fists clenched, ready to release all of its pent-up anger.

Voice rising, he demanded, "Are you accusing me of cheating?"

Chapter 24

"So, Mrs. McCracken, we'll allow him to finish out the remainder of the day, but starting Monday Tyler will receive in-house suspension every day next week," the vice principal, Mr. Ross, said into the phone. "We do not take threats toward our teachers lightly."

Tyler slouched in the chair, glaring at the nameplate on Mr. Ross's desk. He hadn't even really threatened Mr. Hill—although the string of expletives he'd fired at his teacher might have seemed threatening. At that moment he'd felt exactly as he'd felt the whole time he'd been at Riversedge: past the point of ready to explode. Exploding and out of control.

Mr. Ross gave the phone a strange look after he said goodbye to Tyler's mother, most likely marveling at her lack of surprise that Tyler was in trouble again. Then he leaned toward Tyler.

"You need to smarten up," he said, jabbing a finger. "Enough incidents like this will get you expelled."

"Whatever," Tyler muttered.

"You may say 'whatever' now, but you're an intelligent kid, all honors classes. You want to get into college? They don't look kindly on this kind of behavior. You'll find yourself shut out of a future."

Tyler rolled his eyes. What kind of future would he ever have? His girlfriend was possessed by a ghost. If that didn't make him crazy, there was always the fire-setting thing.

Mr. Ross slapped a hall pass down on the desk. "Get out of my office."

Tyler dragged himself to his next class. In the deserted hallway he saw a lone, familiar figure.

"Ty! Hey, man, what's up?" Danny held his palm up for a high five.

"What are you doing in the hallway?"

Awkwardly Danny dropped his hand. "Going to the bathroom." Tyler knew the bathroom was at the other end of the hallway. "Hey, look, about last weekend... Sorry, man. You looked kinda stressed all week so I didn't say anything, but I feel really bad on running out on you..." Danny put on his pathetic face.

Tyler looked him, unmoved. "Whatever."

Accepting this as forgiveness, Danny's face perked up. "Anyway, to make it up to you, I wanted to invite you over tonight. Well, not to my house, exactly." Danny's eyes darted around to see if anyone else was listening. The hallway was still deserted. "But I think you know where I mean." He raised his eyebrows suggestively.

"What are you talking about, Danny?" Tyler was too tired to guess.

"You know, that house. The one we went to last weekend?"

The abandoned house. Tyler gritted his teeth. "What are you talking about, you're inviting me over?"

"Max and his friends really like the place. And since Bobby got in trouble for the party last weekend, I guess the cops showed up and busted a few kids for underage drinking, and I guess a few kids had pot or something, anyway, Max told Bobby about the house and Bobby thought it was an awesome idea to have a party there. You know, because no one knows about it."

"Except all the people your brother invited to the party, right?" Tyler said through his teeth. His rage was coming back.

"Yeah, but not, like, the police," Danny said, completely missing the point.

"I don't think I'll be able to make it." He certainly didn't want to be anywhere near that house tonight. On his calendar at home was a big black circle captioned, "Full Moon."

"That sucks, dude. Jasmine said she might come. I really want you to meet her."

"Sorry."

Tyler wasn't sorry in the least. Danny was exactly like every other person in his life. Ready to abandon him the moment things got rough. His right hand slipped into his pocket. His fingers gripped the smooth plastic casing of the lighter, his thumb resting on the notched wheel. An eerie calm came over him.

***

Tyler dreaded going to lunch. Would Karin sit with her cheerleader friends, or would Ellen choose to sit with Tyler? He dragged his feet until Mike turned and said, "Come on, Tyler, hurry up. It's hamburger day."

Waiting for him in the lunch room, as he knew she would be, Karin had even gone so far as to save a seat for him. He swallowed thickly and walked to her side like a man walking to his execution.

She smiled sweetly. "Hello, Tyler. How was your morning?"

"I got suspended."

He hunched himself over his lunch and tried not to look at her. Or touch her. Or smell her.

Apparently he was very obvious about this, because when Mike got back from the lunch line with a fully loaded burger, he leaned over and murmured in Tyler's ear, "Are you and Karin having problems?"

"You could say that," Tyler said.

"I heard you got suspended again," Mike said, louder this time. "What happened?"

"Mr. Hill accused me of cheating."

"You can't be serious!" Karin exclaimed, clasping her hands to her chest.

Tyler wasn't the only one looking at her strangely.

She cleared her throat. "I mean, you wouldn't do something like that, would you, Tyler?"

"No," Tyler scoffed.

"Of course you wouldn't." Karin returned to her own lunch, a salad perfectly packed in a Tupperware container.

"Of course I wouldn't," Tyler repeated loudly. "Since you were the one who helped me study."

"Me? But I'm terrible at mathematics."

This response brought a chorus of chuckles from the other kids at the table. "Stop playing modest, Karin," said one girl. "You're good at everything."

Tyler allowed the table's conversation to move on without him. This was definitely Ellen sitting beside him, Ellen trying so hard to pretend to be Karin and failing. From the silence coming from his left, he knew she felt embarrassed. He didn't want to humiliate her—even though Ellen was threatening to have him possessed by a ghost, she was still a girl, one who had been abandoned by everyone, too.

And if there was any chance of Ellen leaving Karin's body, he didn't need Karin to find out that he had essentially humiliated her too.

The lunch period was almost over and Tyler was beginning to think he would escape when Karin said, "Tyler, can I speak with you for a moment? Privately?"

One of the guys at the table muttered, "Oooh..."

Tyler cast a glance at Mike and the other guys warning them to shut up, then followed Karin through the sea of empty tables were all the freaks sat. She perched on the windowsill, the light from the windows giving her hair a halo. He leaned on the sill a distance away. His eyes drifted up to the clock.

A cold touch on his arm brought him back to business. "God, your skin is like ice," he said, jerking his arm away.

"What are your plans for this evening?" Karin asked.

"I don't have any plans."

He crossed his arms and glared at the clock. One minute left until the bell.

"Good. Then you'll have no problem meeting me tonight, as per our arrangement."

"You make it sound so polite," he muttered.

"There's no need for rudeness."

"Oh, so if I don't show up, it's because I'm rude?"

"I would strongly suggest you show up. Midnight would be the ideal time." Karin hopped off the sill and smoothed her skirt at the same time the bell rang. She leaned in and whispered with a cold breath into his ear, "I shouldn't like to see what she'll do to you if you break your promise."

Her golden hair swung behind her prettily as she strolled out of the cafeteria.

It wasn't until Tyler saw Danny riding his bike home from school that the coldness crept into his stomach. All those kids were going to be at the house when Lily came out to take over his body.

Chapter 25

Tyler's flashlight beam bounced along ahead of him as he stormed through the forest. Part of him hoped Danny's brothers had changed their minds and decided not to have a party. He hadn't even reached the road when he could hear the music, and see the lights. He hoped they weren't stupid enough to bring any fireworks.

It hadn't been hard sneaking out of his house. His parents had been ignoring him all evening. Would they even notice when some sicko ghost had possessed him?

Grimly he thought, Maybe they'll like her better.

A collection of four wheelers and dirt bikes were scattered in the road in front of the house. Tyler wove his way through them and walked in through the open kitchen door. He could barely believe what he saw.

Coleman lanterns sat on the countertops and flashlights dangled from the ceiling. There was a keg in a bucket of ice near the door. Tyler was relieved to see that the basement door was closed, but he knew from the lights outside that at least Ellen's bedroom was occupied.

He walked into the living room, searching for Danny. Some girls bumped into him on their way to the kitchen, and one of them sneered, "Who invited the freshman?" The other girl giggled.

Through the office doorway, Tyler could see three kids with axes hacking up the desk. He pushed his way in and demanded, "What are you doing?"

"Getting firewood, duh," said one of the kids. He swung and splintered off a piece of the top, then threw it into a pile.

"You can't do that," Tyler said.

A few of the guys laughed. "Yeah, whatever kid. This desk has been sitting here for, like, fifty years. I don't think anyone's going to miss it."

Another kid shoved Tyler aside on his way into the room. "You want me to put some of this into the fireplace?"

"Yeah."

Tyler turned away, feeling helpless. There were too many of them to scream for them to get out like he'd done last time, too many guys who could beat the crap out of him.

The house shuddered with each axe swing.

He made his way upstairs, pushing past a couple making out. With relief, Tyler saw that the door to the black hole room was still closed, but when he got to Ellen's doorway, he stopped dead.

Candles covered every surface, their flames dancing in the drafts. Danny, Max, some girl all dressed in black with a necklace shaped like a pentagram, and a few other people were seated on the floor in a tight circle. They all had their eyes closed, but only the goth girl had her face lifted. "Come to us, spirits," she intoned. "Come, speak to us spirits. We call you." A step closer revealed a Ouija board.

"What are you doing?" Tyler screamed, taking two steps and kicking at the Ouija board. "Are you crazy?"

The goth girl opened her eyes and glared at Tyler through her eyeliner.

"What are YOU doing?" demanded one of the girls. "Who do you think you are?"

"Yeah, kid. Get lost," said a boy who was clearly her boyfriend.

"No way. This is my house," Tyler said without thinking. His face burned when the kids started laughing. Not Danny, who shrank back and looked at his brother with wide eyes.

"You know, I told Danny not to invite you," said Max, standing up. "I know you'd flip out like this. Maybe you don't think I know what a freak you are, but I do."

"What are you talking about?" Tyler snarled.

"Come on, don't you remember me? Maybe not, I used to have a Mohawk, and I was only there a week or so before they sent me to lock up. I was at that stupid 'treatment center' with you. You were one of the fire-setters. A little twerp, and you used to freak out all the time. One of the days I was there you had to get restrained like five times."

"You were there?" A memory swam to back Tyler, of a lanky kid with a mohawk swaggering into the room. Too many memories of that place had to do with group therapy and punching the walls and having the staff tackle him to the ground to stop him from hitting the other kids. During his years there, he had seen so many other boys come and go, each one making him progressively angrier. He tried to swallow that down. "How come you were there?"

"I brought a knife to school. But I'm not an idiot like you were. I played it cool, did exactly what the therapist said, and when I got to court everyone said I was fine. You, on the other hand, were a mental case. Still are, as far as I can see. Look, you're getting all pissed."

Tyler tried to unclench his fists, to show he could control his anger.

Instead he launched himself at Max, punching anything and everything in his way.

Hands grabbed at him, voices yelled at him to stop. He barely got a few good punches on Max before Max's friends had him restrained.

"See," Max huffed, leaning against Ellen's vanity, "you are crazy."

In response, Tyler kicked at him. Two more of Max's friends grabbed Tyler's legs. Tyler struggled, but they were much bigger and stronger than he was.

"Come on, guys," Max said. "Let's put him in solitary. Danny, grab that chair there."

Tyler couldn't see if Danny grabbed the chair or not. He knew better than to depend on Danny to have his back. As they carried him downstairs, Tyler struggled every step of the way, but Max and his friends held tight. The crowd in the living room parted to let them through. "He's going to solitary!" Max announced, and a cheer went up in response.

"Screw you!" Tyler yelled at them.

The guys chopping up the desk raised their axes like a salute.

They entered the kitchen. "Danny, open the basement door," Max ordered.

"Max, you can't put him down there..." Danny ventured.

Max lifted up one foot and shoved Danny in the back with it. "Just do it! Or you'll go down with him!"

Danny shifted from one foot to the other nervously. "But Max..."

"Do it!"

Tyler closed his eyes and prayed that Danny would stand up to his brother. He prayed that after Danny had pledged himself as Tyler's best friend, that Danny could help him. The disappointment already filled him.

Instead of being released, Tyler heard the basement door creak open. He opened his eyes to see it waiting for him like a big hungry mouth.

His only chance to escape was when they put him down. He waited for that moment, but instead of letting him go and shoving him in, they threw him. The door slammed and closed out all but a sliver of light.

Tyler was flying through darkness, with no reference point to understand if he was falling or simply floating. He waited for his body to hit the stairs, but time seemed to have slowed down. He was floating, not falling. For a fleeting moment he lost all fear of hitting the ground.

Then the stairs slammed into his back.

He tumbled down and down. He spread out his arms and legs to try to find a purchase somewhere, to stop the downward motion. Finally he hit the bottom and lay there, his lungs locked until he forced himself to breathe painfully. His breaths came in short, high-pitched gasps.

Eventually he caught his breath and he was able to sit up. His entire body hurt. He felt hard swollen knots on his arms, on his hips and knees. He rested his back against the cobwebby cold stone wall.

They were up there, laughing like nothing had happened, like it was cool to hurl a kid down a flight of stairs. Tyler's anger flared again, and he found himself on his feet and pacing. He wasn't stupid enough to punch these stone walls. He kept one hand touching the wall as he paced, a reminder of the fear he'd felt the last time he'd been in the basement, but otherwise his anger had swallowed everything. He ran his hand along all the stones, occasionally kicking one and bruising his toes inside his sneaker.

The music thumped, then the scent of burning wood drifted down to Tyler's nose.

He wondered if they were so stupid that they would start a fire in the fireplace of a house built with wood as dry as tinder, with a chimney that was most likely clogged with debris or leaves. He wandered into the middle of the cellar, trying to determine which part of the ceiling corresponded with the fireplace. He smelled smoke clear as day. "Stupid idiots," he growled, and started toward the stairs to go up and bang on the door and tell them how stupid they were.

His feet kicked a pile of something. It felt like a pile of swept up dirt and wood pieces, like in his dad's workshop. He took out his lighter, flicked the flint. Once his eyes adjusted to the bright flame, he squatted down and held the light out over the mess.

White bits of what looked like bone poked out of the dust.

Tyler jerked away and lost the light.

His hands fumbled, trying to get the light back, then stopped. Were his eyes adjusting to the darkness?

No.

The stones were... glowing.

He spun around, staring at the eerie blue light emanating from the five stones that made up the basement walls.

Five?

"I'm pleased to see that you changed your mind."

The voice drifted out of the increasingly bright darkness. From between two of the stones, Karin stepped—glided, really. She was practically translucent.

How much of Karin was actually left?

"It's very noble that you decided to sacrifice yourself instead of your sister, or one of the souls upstairs." She floated closer, bringing with her a cloud of icy air. "Lily was unsure before, but now she sees how black your soul is."

A crushing weight pressed Tyler to the floor, although nothing was touching him that he could tell. He pushed against it, but it covered every inch of his skin at once, like an iron blanket.

Then he saw the shoes.

If he could have backed away, run screaming, he would have. Instead, he felt his face forced down to the cold dirt floor.

One black shoe slid forward, revealing a black stocking and the hem of a black dress.

"No!" he screamed, or tried to. His voice seemed to freeze in the air. "Please, don't!"

"It won't hurt, Tyler," Ellen assured him. "She's already inside of you. She's been inside of you since you first arrived."

The other shoe moved forward. His lungs were frozen, he couldn't breathe—

"All it takes is one little weakness. She likes that, the weakness, the rotten parts of the fruit. She eats it, gobbles it right up." With the darkness creeping in around his vision, he couldn't see anymore, but somehow Ellen's dimpled smile was right there in front of him. "It makes you feel good. You liked what she did to you, and that's why you kept coming back here."

"Nooo..." he moaned.

"Karin was weak too, but not as weak as you. Karin is perfect for me. But Lily is so ancient... When I called her forth from the stones I was afraid, just like you are now. She took my parents, as I wanted, but they were like your friend Karin. Too good and pure. I was afraid when she took me, too, but see? Now we are friends forever."

"Your parents..." Tyler gasped. "Your parents killed you."

Ellen's laugh echoed against the stones. "No, Tyler, I killed them, with Lily's help. When you're weak, you can make a person believe anything."

"You... were never... sick?"

"Boys," Ellen said, shaking her head. "So easy to manipulate."

A low laughing moan seemed to agree with her.

Tyler couldn't force himself to breathe anymore. The darkness seemed so... easy.

He closed his eyes.

Chapter 26

"Tyler?"

His eyes cracked open. Could that really be...

Danny?

"I'm down here," he croaked.

"No you're not," Danny said, his voice not so far away anymore.

Tyler sat up. He felt no heaviness, no resistance. He could breathe. He could even see a little. They were outside the house. The windows blazed with light and smoke filled the air, but Tyler could still see and hear the party going on inside.

"I carried you out of the basement all by myself." Danny's chest was puffed up with pride. "Not even Max could stop me."

"What about Karin?"

"What about her?"

"Is she still in the basement?"

Danny stared at him. "Dude, there wasn't anyone down there with you. Did you hit your head?"

"No, Karin was down there!" Tyler said. He tried to stand up, but Danny pressed down on his shoulders. "We have to go back!"

"We can't. Max kicked me out."

Tyler relaxed and stared at the ground. Something nagged at his memory. He shook his head. "I guess I'll head home then."

"Do you want me to walk with you?" In the darkness Danny's eyes were big and hopeful.

"No, I'm fine." Tyler turned his back on Danny, trying not to see the defeat in his friend's shoulders. No, it was best if Danny was left out of this completely.

***

Tyler eased his back door open and crept up to his room. The only sound he heard was his father's loud and rhythmical snoring.

His bedside lamp created a little pool of light. There was the book, right where he had left it. He flipped through the grotesque pages until his eyes caught on the drawing he was looking for.

Beneath a diagram of a pentagram, inked representations of stones stood in a circle. It reminded Tyler of Stonehenge. Some people thought Stonehenge held some ancient power –the formation of the circle or in the stones themselves, or the location of the circle on a ley line, Tyler didn't know. But he didn't care so much about Stonehenge as what the stones reminded him of: another book, slightly newer.

Local Ghost Stories and Legends of Middlebury County.

When the townspeople had gone up to the forest where the girls had seen apparitions, they found a circle of stones. They thought the stones, in their formation, had something to do with the apparitions and the witchcraft, and they had moved the stones out of the circle to break their power.

Tyler had a feeling that these were the stones Ellen's father had used for the foundation of his house.

Part of him wanted to go back to the life he had before and pretend he'd never discovered the house. Lily didn't seem to be able to leave the house, and if she'd somehow missed taking possession of him while he was down in that basement, all the better for him. He could stay away from the house. Lily couldn't possess him if he never went back.

But there was Karin.

He didn't know if she was trapped in that basement, but she was trapped with Ellen walking around wearing her body. He was sure that if she had any conscious thought left, Karin would want him to save her.

He stared down at the illustration. The strange, old-fashioned typeset and the Latin words of the text snagged his eye. He didn't know if it was a spell or something else, and if it was a spell, it might not even be an exorcism kind of spell. It might actually make everything worse.

If it didn't work, he needed a backup plan. He needed a way to destroy Lily and the Birdsall house. And Ellen, and maybe Karin.

He wasn't so sure he could make it out alive, either, if he had to resort to the idea now coming to him.

He slid the book into the waistband of his jeans, trying not to think about that oily skin paper touching him. He shut off his light and slipped back downstairs and out into the garage.

All he needed was some gasoline. There had to be some, for the lawn mower, for the snow blower. He turned on his phone's flashlight and scanned for a red plastic gasoline can. Fire would destroy the house and the spirits in it. He ransacked the shelves as quietly as possible, but couldn't find anything remotely resembling a gas can. A lock secured a large plastic storage trunk, the only place that gas can could be. "Damn it!" he muttered. Of course his parents would go that far. The only thing he found remotely flammable was a pint-size tin can of turpentine.

In the middle of the garage, Tyler's four-wheeler couldn't help but attract his attention. There was gas in the tank, maybe he could drain it, along with the lawnmower's gas tank. Although...

Fire wouldn't do much to destroy the stones. Maybe falling timbers from the house would knock them over, but what he really needed were explosives.

Tyler lifted the helmet from the four-wheeler's handlebars and put it on, then grabbed his dad's hiking backpack from a hook and put the turpentine inside. He knew where he could go to get what he needed.

Of course, his new plan also involved somehow getting the garage door open and starting up the four-wheeler without waking up his parents. He sat for long minutes, trying to figure out how to sneak out.

No matter what he did, they'd hear him leave. No matter how his plan went, he was going to be in trouble after tonight. He cracked his neck and took a deep breath, then hit the garage door opener. As it was rumbling open, he revved the four-wheeler and took off, ducking under the half-open door. Soon he was out of the garage and in the woods.

It took him a little longer than he'd thought to find the trails that would lead him anywhere near Danny's house, especially in the dark. The headlights of the four-wheeler didn't illuminate much. He had to be careful crossing the streets, and hoped that anyone living in the houses near where he was riding wouldn't call the cops. Good thing Danny's house was out in the middle of nowhere.

Just beyond the tree line of the Krull property, Tyler shut off the four-wheeler. He could see his target: the shed. A flickering light on the first floor of the house meant someone was probably asleep in front of the television. Tyler moved across the backyard stealthily, only once tripping over a tire hidden in the grass. The light from the window actually helped.

Tyler got to the shed and pulled at the door handle. It didn't open. Tyler looked at the lock holding the door closed. What was he going to do without the key? Maybe he could pry out the screws holding the latch and get in that way.

His fingernails didn't quite fit into the screws. Tyler started looking around on the ground for something, a screwdriver, or spare change.

Maybe he could do something with the hinges. He stood up to examine them.

A soft step behind him was his only warning before he was tackled from behind.

"Argh!" Tyler yelled, but his voice was muffled because it was full of grass and dirt.

"I've got you now!"

Tyler managed to turn his head to the side and spit out some weeds. "Danny! Get off of me!"

"Tyler?"

The weight came off Tyler's back and he rolled over, looked at Danny in the moonlight.

"Sorry," Danny said sheepishly. "I thought you were... you know... That thing from the basement."

Tyler sat up and rubbed the grass and leaves out of his hair. "What thing?"

"I don't know. It was black, and it was standing over you, and it freaked me out. But when I shone my flashlight at it, it disappeared." Danny rubbed the back of his head, looking embarrassed. Danny didn't seem to notice that Tyler could barely breathe. Lily, Tyler thought. That black thing was Lily. With an awkward laugh, Danny said, "Probably I imagined the whole thing. So what are you doing out here? It's almost midnight."

"Midnight?" Tyler hadn't looked at his phone, but the last time he had checked, it had barely been ten. He had thought he had an hour or more to get his plan set up. He jumped up.

"You gotta be somewhere?" Danny joked.

Tyler looked at Danny, considering, before deciding he'd have to tell Danny what was going on if he wanted to get inside the shed. "Yeah. I need to go blow that house up. Can I borrow some fireworks?"

"Really? Man, when Max said you were a pyro, I didn't really believe him—"

Tyler blinked. "Wait, Max was the one who told you?"

"Yeah, on the first day of school. He pointed you out and said, 'Hey, I know that kid. That kid's a total pyro.' I figured if I had a cool friend like you, maybe Max would stop picking on me so much."

Tyler remembered what Danny's brother had said back at the house. "Max doesn't seem to think I'm so cool."

"Yeah, well. You're still a good friend."

There was a moment of awkward silence.

"Hey! So is that why you were trying to break into my shed? To steal fireworks?"

"Yeah. Do you have the key?"

"I can go get it!" Danny dashed for the house. Tyler slipped back and hid in the shadows behind the shed. Danny had better not wake up his whole family.

Minutes later, Danny launched across the yard.

"I got it!"

Danny fumbled with the lock, then pulled open the shed door. A loud squeal echoed in the night. Both boys froze. When nothing happened, they entered the shed. "How much do you need?" Danny asked. There were still dozens of boxes of fireworks left.

"Well, I can't carry more than one or two boxes," Tyler said. "And I'm not sure how I'll fit them on my four-wheeler."

"You have a four-wheeler?" Danny yelled.

"Shh!"

"You have a four-wheeler?" Danny whispered.

"Yes, I got it for my birthday. I didn't tell you?"

"No!"

"Well, I got a four-wheeler, and that's how I got here. It's parked out in the woods."

"Show me!"

"At least help me carry a few boxes out there," Tyler complained. "You don't have any dynamite in here, do you?"

Danny stared at him.

"I think these will work fine."

The boys headed across the yard hefting two boxes each.

"Where is it? Where is it?" Danny asked.

Tyler didn't know how Danny could have so much energy. Tyler himself had been feeling okay, but now... now it seemed like his adrenaline rush had worn off. His feet dragged. "Over there."

Danny bounded ahead. Out of the darkness Danny's whisper sounded louder than it should have. "This is freaking awesome!"

Tyler finally got to the four-wheeler, already worried about how he would carry the boxes while driving, but Danny had solved part of the problem. He had packed Mr. McCracken's backpack with a ridiculous amount of explosives, shoving any left from the first box into the second.

"I'll sit behind you and hold this," Danny said.

Tyler hadn't been planning on Danny coming with him, but maybe Danny would be helpful for the rest of the plan, too. He considered Danny's suggestion. "If you're holding boxes, how are you going to hold on when I start driving?"

Danny grinned and held up a circular object. "I brought duct tape."

***

It was ridiculous. Tyler sat as far up as he could, the hub of the handlebars pressed uncomfortably between his legs. Danny, wearing the backpack, sat behind Tyler, with the box between them. They had passed the roll of duct-tape around Tyler's front and Danny's back, around and around.

"Do you feel secure?" Tyler asked, unable to see if Danny had any part of his butt on the seat of the four-wheeler.

"Uh, yeah," Danny said in a not-very-reassuring way. "Yeah, I'm good."

Tyler started the engine and hit the gas, then had to immediately stop so Danny could right himself. He was sweating despite the cool autumn night. He could already be too late. Lily might have found some other victim to possess.

"Let go of the box," Tyler said over his shoulder. "Just hold my waist or something." Danny released his grip on the box, since it was safely wedged between them, and grabbed Tyler's sweatshirt in his fists. This felt better. "Let's go," he said.

The four-wheeler kicked up dirt behind him as they sped off down the dark trails.

Soon he was crossing Pine Hill Road and heading up Birdsall Drive, mowing down all the weeds and baby trees in his way. The house party was still going strong. Tyler slowed to a stop as smoothly as he could, but Danny's weight forced the box to slam into his spine. Tyler grunted and turned off the vehicle.

Without the roaring engine in his ears, the pumping music was deafening. And Danny's yelps as he slid to the side. "Help!" Danny squealed.

Tyler ignored him, extricating himself from the duct tape and letting Danny topple to the ground. He had other things to worry about. He wrestled the backpack from Danny and put it on.

"Hey, wait for me!" Danny said.

Grabbing the box of fireworks, Tyler said, "There's no time. I have to save Karin!"

Then he ran toward the house, armed to the gills with fireworks.

The kitchen door was still jammed open. He had a clear shot to the basement.

Then he tripped over the doorstop. The box in his hands went flying as he did a full face plant on the floor. A slam behind him told him he wasn't alone.

"What are you doing back here, freak?"

Max's voice.

"And what is all this?"

Tyler felt a hand on the back of his head, then the fingers grasped his hair and pulled. He scrambled with his feet so his hair didn't pull clean out of his head.

"You want to go back in the basement?"

Instead of the beer Tyler expected to smell on Max's breath, he instead smelled something rotting and ancient. Max's eyes flashed black.

Lily had found a new soul to feed on.

Chapter 27

Max hauled Tyler along by the hair, and Tyler tripped over the fallen box, kicking it to the side and spilling fireworks all over the floor. Everyone backed away to let Max through, laughing and calling out encouragement: Yeah, get his ass, Max! Show him who's boss!

No one seemed to realize that Max had changed.

The black maw of the basement door loomed ever closer, until Max thrust Tyler up against the doorframe, that stinking breath in Tyler's face. "It's midnight," Max said. His low voice crawled from his throat, so oily Tyler could practically see it. An oily slug-like thing, filtering into Tyler's lungs.

"Please, don't let her do this," he whispered, gagging on the last word.

Dangling on the precipice of the basement stairs, he heard a noise came up from the depths, a keening, primeval sound that Tyler instinctively recognized deep in his bones, in his genetic memory.

Pure evil.

Tyler's vision pulsed with blackness.

"Let him go," came Danny's voice, pure and strong.

Max's mouth curled into a sinister smile. "Sure thing, little bro," he said, and released his grip on Tyler's hair.

Tyler lurched for the doorframe. He caught himself for just a moment, clinging with his fingertips, but the weight of the backpack on his shoulders was pulling him down. Then Max grabbed Danny by the arm and Danny crashed into Tyler and they both fell. Limbs tangled and stairs slammed into his ribs, his legs, his head.

From somewhere up above them, Max said gleefully, "Looks like we'll be having a fireworks show in the backyard!" Cheers went up, and the basement door slammed shut.

Then the floor hit him in the face and everything went black.

Tyler wasn't sure how much time had passed when he finally woke up on the basement floor. Danny was already awake, making pathetic sniffling sounds. Tyler reached out in the dark to find him.

"I think I broke my arm," Danny whimpered.

The darkness pressed against him, but he pushed back. He wasn't sure exactly why he was able to move at all, unless Lily hadn't managed to complete the possession. Maybe it was like Ellen had said, and he had been possessed by Lily ever since he first set foot in the house. It was a struggle to reach his shoulders and shrug off the backpack. Another slow battle to pull the lighter from his pocket.

He wasn't sure if Danny could tell what Tyler was doing until Danny said, "I have a couple cherry bombs in my pocket."

"You do?"

"Yeah... I had them before... thought maybe everyone would think they were cool... Do you think they'll help?"

***

As Tyler ascended the stairs, holding Danny up with one arm, he let the turpentine he'd packed in the bottom of the backpack dribble out of the can, only a little on each step. He hoped it would be enough. By the time he got to the top, the can was empty.

"See if you can get the door open, okay?" Tyler said.

Danny nodded, clutching his arm.

Returning to the bottom of the stairs, Tyler dropped the can, letting the metallic sound echo. The stones were giving off that faint glow again, but he couldn't see anyone in the basement with him.

"Ellen?" he called quietly. "Karin?"

"I'm here," Ellen said, stepping out of the darkness. Her skin was luminous, her eyes huge. "Have you come to be with me? Forever?"

Tyler swallowed. It made a dry click in his throat. Then he held out his hand. "Yes."

Ellen's face relaxed into a smile, that smile he'd fallen in love with, back when it belonged to Karin. "Maybe it won't be so bad," she said. "If you're a boy. I've never had a boyfriend."

She took his hand.

She was talking to him like he was already Lily, but he didn't have time to think about that. He yanked Ellen's hand so had she stumbled forward.

"What are you doing?" Ellen cried.

"I'm helping you." He hoped Karin, somewhere under Ellen's control, would realize he was talking to her. "Let's go."

He fumbled in his pocket for the lighter, dragging Ellen toward the stairs.

"What are you doing?" Ellen screamed. "What are you doing?"

With the lighter in his grasp, he thumbed the flint once, twice, three times before the little flame popped up.

When she saw the fire, Ellen's eyes grew wide. "Tyler? You would do this to me? You would... kill me?"

Tyler hesitated when she said that. "I'm not killing you."

"You are," she said. "If you destroy this house, you will kill me."

He hoped she meant only Ellen would die, but he had to take the chance that she meant something else. Keeping her in his grasp, he bent over and touched the lighter to the fluid.

Immediately the house wailed, a scream flew toward his head that didn't come from Ellen. He ducked, but knew he didn't have much time. Hoisting Ellen over his shoulder, he started running up the stairs. Danny had opened the door for him. The rectangle of light beckoned to him.

The scream came again, knocking him into the wall.

He ran like he'd never run before. He'd never had anything to run for, nothing like this. His feet flew. The door, the finish line, it tantalized him, this white pure light. He made for it, faster than he'd ever run, even with Karin on his back.

The door wavered, seeming to grow further and further away.

An illusion. It was all an illusion, created by Lily or some force in the stones, he didn't know which. He didn't care. He squeezed his eyes shut and kept running. His heart beat like it would burst but still he ran, waiting to feel the heat at his back. Waiting for a reddish tint on his eyelids, waiting for the sweet smell of smoke and chemicals and a whoosh of air and fire.

He waited, and when he finally tumbled through the doorway into the kitchen, onto the mess of fuses and fireworks, it still hadn't come.

Kids were standing around staring at him, smoke coming up through the rotting floorboards beneath their feet.

He turned and looked down at the black hole. He gasped for air.

"Run!" he yelled at them.

His voice seemed to cut through the fog that held them captive. "Fire!" someone yelled, and the stampede began.

"Let me go!" Ellen screamed, and beat at him with her fists.

Tyler removed one of the cherry bombs from his pocket, dodging Ellen's weak blows. He flicked the lighter and held it to the end of the fuse. The fuse caught and hissed. Then he tossed it down the stairs as if it were a whiffle ball.

"Get out! Can't you see, this place is gonna catch on fire!" Danny's voice came from the living room. "Get out!"

Tyler sucked in a breath and called, "Danny, get outside!"

The floorboards thrummed with running footsteps. Kids shoved their way out of the house, knocking into each other, shoving at the kitchen door until one of the hinges gave way.

Suddenly Ellen was beating him with both fists. She was pushing him toward the basement, screaming unintelligibly. He didn't have much time. He turned to face her, taking her blows to his chest, and grabbed her over his shoulder again. Only a few steps to the door.

He had his hand on the door knob when the cherry bomb exploded. There was a satisfying crack—a wail as the power of the stones was broken.

The floor shuddered under his feet. He wobbled and regained his balance. Danny was right there. Tyler shoved Ellen into his arms and turned to throw the remaining firecrackers in the general vicinity of the basement. The heat was coming, racing up the stairs.

For a moment Tyler was mesmerized. He couldn't look away. He had to see the fire.

It was Danny who pulled him away from the door, who got both Tyler and Ellen out of the house and behind someone's Jeep.

The explosion of all the firecrackers was deafening.

Cartwheels of fire shot off inside the house. Red, green, and blue sparks erupted and caught on the rags of curtains in the windows. That noise, that awful noise, it didn't die under the roaring of the fire and the intermittent pops of the explosives.

The horrible wailing got louder and louder until that was all Tyler could hear.

Suddenly Tyler felt something stuck in his throat. He gagged, dropping the book and dropping to his knees. The feeling was horrible; it was like his insides were trying to exit his body through his throat. Tears came to his eyes and his stomach heaved, trying to get it out.

A long black snakelike thing slithered out through his teeth. His eyes bugged out—he couldn't breathe—his stomach heaved and heaved and the thing slowly flowed out of him. He couldn't breathe, and black dots blinked in front of his eyes. He blinked, the tears coming faster now.

The black thing finally dropped out of his mouth and onto the dirty floor, and finally Tyler was able to vomit. His stomach clenched. He felt so weak... the smoke was rising, encapsulating him, until everything was black.

Chapter 28

When he woke up, he was back in the basement. Only it wasn't dark, it was light, and flames were devouring the stairs, his only escape. He dodged bits of burning wood that rained down on him. He screamed for Sam, he screamed for Danny. The heat enveloped him, his entire body was sweating, he was drenched. He screamed for those he knew, then he screamed for anyone, someone, to please help him, he would do anything. He screamed until he lost all hope, then he screamed some more.

He could see her watching him from the shadows.

"You belong to me now," Lily's rotting vocal chords hissed. Her black shoe slid into the brightness of the flames, and he saw the hem of her dress.

His head jerked, his body spasmed. Strong hands held him down.

"You're okay, kid, you're okay."

Tyler's eyes felt glued shut, but the air he breathed was clean and cool. No smoke, he realized. No dank basement smell. On the backs of his eyelids, lights flashed, red and blue.

He peeled his eyes open. He was in the back of an ambulance, on a gurney. He reached up and touched the oxygen mask pressed to his face.

"What's going on?" he croaked. His throat burned.

Beside him a man in a blue collared shirt was staring out the back of the ambulance, where a cluster of EMTs were standing and talking to kids who looked freaked out, blankets over their shoulders. Tyler didn't know any of them. "They're getting the fire under control," the EMT beside Tyler said. He pulled out a penlight and shone it in each of Tyler's eyes, making Tyler wince.

Distantly Tyler heard the roar of the fire. He closed his eyes, imagining the Birdsall house completely engulfed in flames. With the stone foundation blown to pieces, it was only a matter of time before it all collapsed.

He closed his eyes in relief.

"Where's Danny? And Karin?" he asked.

Before the EMT could answer, a voice crackled over the radio at his hip. "Get names from those kids before you get them out of here. We need to clear this area to get more trucks in."

Now Tyler could see police officers among the kids clustered in the road. They were taking down names, asking questions. Some of the kids were pointing towards Tyler. He didn't see Danny or Karin among them. Or Max.

"Your friends are fine," the EMT said, reaching out to close the door of the ambulance. "We gotta get you to the hospital."

"But how do I know they're fine?" Tyler asked, struggling to sit up. His stomach muscles screamed at him.

The EMT pushed him back. Tyler was too weak to resist, and his head flopped back against the gurney. "The firefighters got everyone out. Don't worry."

Tyler couldn't quite think of how to ask if Danny or Karin seemed like themselves. "But how do I know they're fine?" he mumbled.

No one answered him.

***

When Tyler's parents showed up in the door of his hospital room, he barely recognized them. It was nearly three a.m. and he had been half-asleep since he'd been checked over by the nurses and given a room, and his parents looked like they had been through as much as he had. They had drawn, worried faces, and their hair looked grayer than ever. Tyler held his breath, waiting to see if the first words out of their mouths would be that the cops had contacted them and he was heading back to juvie.

Instead, they both looked like they had been crying, and his mother was smiling at him.

"Hi," he croaked through his oxygen mask.

His mother gave a little sob and hugged him. "Oh, Tyler," was all she said.

Cautiously, he put his arms around her.

He waited for them to say the words he dreaded.

We're going to get you some help. Obviously this is too big a problem to ignore.

Or, The police told us what you did. How could you do this, Tyler?

Mrs. McCracken pulled back and wiped her face. "The doctor said you were okay?" she said, her voice lilting like it was a question. "You had some smoke inhalation and some bruising but you're okay?"

"Yeah." He looked at his dad, hoping for a clue. His dad had never been easy to read, though, and now was no exception. "Can I go home now?"

"They want to keep you for observation until the morning," Mrs. McCracken said. "And the police want to interview you, but that can wait until you're discharged."

Tyler winced, waiting for his parents to start in.

We know you started that fire.

Tyler gulped a breath. If the police wanted to interrogate him, that meant they knew he had started the fire in the Birdsall house. This was going to be worse than the fire in the warehouse. Way worse. It was his second offense. He steeled himself, waiting for his parents to tell him more.

Mrs. McCracken sighed and looked at Tyler's dad. His parents had a whole conversation in that glance between them. Tyler could only guess at what they were saying to each other.

This is all your fault, you gave him that four-wheeler.

We should have kept him in therapy.

How much is the lawyer going to cost this time?

Finally, his father spoke. "Your friend Danny told us how you carried that girl out of that house."

Tyler shook his head, trying to process what his father was saying. "Danny?" When had Danny spoken to his parents? What did Danny have to do with any of this?

"Yes, the boy in the waiting room with the broken arm. The hospital discharged him but he refused to leave and his mother just left him here, poor thing. He's been out there all night." Mr. McCracken shook his head. "He said the older boys had locked you all in the basement, and your friend Karin had gotten hurt, and when the fire started you carried her out."

Somehow Tyler hadn't gotten past his parents talking about Danny to the girl he had carried out of the house. He lurched up and tried to pull down his oxygen mask. "Karin? Is Karin okay?"

His mother pushed at him to lie back down and repositioned the oxygen mask.

"She's fine, Tyler." Mr. McCracken cleared his throat. "Danny also said his brother was the one who started the fire."

Here it was. Here was where they said they didn't believe a word of it.

"Is that true?" Mrs. McCracken asked.

Tyler pulled away. Tell his parents the truth, and risk them sending him to the mental hospital. He barely believed it all himself.

But Max had played a big part in why Tyler had started the fire. Max had set off a bunch of fireworks, too.

Tyler looked down at the hospital bracelet on his wrist. "Max was at Riversedge with me," he said, and that was all his parents needed.

"I knew that family was bad news," his mother said. "I don't want you hanging around with that boy anymore."

He could let his parents forbid him from hanging out with Danny. A few weeks ago, he might have let them. But now he imagined Danny sitting out in the waiting room with a fresh cast on his arm, bruises on his face, hoping for word that Tyler was all right. He remembered how Danny had launched himself at his own brother to help a friend.

"Danny isn't like Max," Tyler said. "I wouldn't have gotten out of that house without him."

Mrs. McCracken huffed, but nodded. "He does seem very concerned about you."

"But what about Karin?" Tyler asked.

"She looked fine when we saw her," Mr. McCracken said. "A little confused, but the nurse seemed to think it was smoke inhalation."

They didn't know what had happened at the house, and Tyler's tired brain was already starting to wonder if it had all been something he imagined. He needed to talk to Karin himself to be sure, but then his parents suggesting letting Danny see him. When Danny's miserable face appeared in the doorway, Tyler couldn't help but quirk a smile at him. "How's your arm?" he croaked.

"Hurts like hell," Danny said, then glanced apologetically at Tyler's parents. "Sorry."

"I'm sure it does hurt. Do you need a ride home?" Mr. McCracken asked.

"Yeah, that'd be great!" Danny said. Tyler's parents headed into the hallway, and Danny hurried to Tyler's bedside. "Dude, you almost died!"

"I would have, if you didn't help me," Tyler said. He knew the tightness in his throat wasn't from the fire. "You're my best friend."

"Aw, bro, you're my best friend, too!" Danny snaked his non-broken arm around Tyler's neck, avoiding all the tubes. "We should get matching tats when we turn eighteen."

"Sure," Tyler said, because that was a lot of years away. But also because it was kinda cool to have a friend like Danny. No one else would ever believe what had happened. Danny knew. Danny believed. And that was something Tyler didn't think anyone else would ever understand.

***

Between more tests at the hospital and getting discharged and the interview at the police station that went alarmingly well, Tyler was ready to crash once he got home. As his dad's car pulled into the driveway, he saw someone familiar waiting for him on the front porch.

"Karin!" he called as soon as his dad put the car in park.

She grinned at him and waved, smiling her old smile. He bounded up to her and just barely stopped himself from hugging her. With a glance back at his parents, he held out his hand and they awkwardly shook hands. Her skin looked less pale, and her hair gleamed golden in the autumn sunlight.

"We'll give you two some privacy," his mother said with a wink as she and Tyler's dad headed inside.

Karin watched them go, making sure the door closed before whispering, "Did you have to talk to the police?" she asked, a worried line between her eyebrows. "Are you in trouble?"

"I don't think so," Tyler said. "Danny told them Max started the fire, so I'm pretty sure I'm not in trouble. I feel kinda bad, though... Max is probably going to end up back in juvie, and it's all my fault."

"But he was setting off fireworks, right?" Karin said. "One spark could have set that house on fire."

In the sunlight, Karin looked so much like her old self, the girl he could never stop smiling around. He wondered what she remembered from the time when she was possessed. "Do you remember any of it?" he asked. "The police talked to you, too, right?"

"I don't remember much." She shrugged with a little grin. "It's probably just as well. I'm just glad you're okay, Tyler." Reaching out, she grabbed his hand and squeezed it.

"Yeah, it's probably for the best," he sighed. "Still, I hate that Max is going to take all the blame. Some stuff he did was bad, but other stuff..." Tyler thought about Max's dark eyes and how most of what he did the night before was probably Lily's doing.

Karin pulled him closer and leaned in. "Max deserves whatever he gets," she said, and the tone of her voice, some dark vibration, made Tyler pull away and really look at her.

She was smiling at him like nothing was wrong.

And the longer he looked at her, tried to see if some other being was under there, wearing her skin, peering out through her eyes, the more certain he became that Karin wasn't simply Karin.

Perhaps Lily was just better at pretending to be Karin than Ellen had been...

CPSIA information can be obtained
at www.ICGtesting.com
Printed in the USA
LVHW081248101122
732762LV00014B/797

9 781804 779309